Dover Thrift Study Edition

Twelfth Night
Or, What You Will

WILLIAM SHAKESPEARE

DOVER PUBLICATIONS, INC.
Mineola, New York

Copyright

Bibliographical Note

This Dover edition, first published in 2010, contains the unabridged text of *Twelfth Night; or, What You Will* as published in Volume VI of *The Caxton Edition of the Complete Works of William Shakespeare,* Caxton Publishing Company, London, n.d., plus literary analysis and perspectives from *MAXnotes® for Twelfth Night,* published in 1996 by Research & Education Association, Inc., Piscataway, New Jersey. The explanatory footnotes to the text of the play were prepared for the Dover edition.

International Standard Book Number

ISBN-13: 978-0-486-47806-7
ISBN-10: 0-486-47806-8

Manufactured in the United States by Courier Corporation
47806801
www.doverpublications.com

Publisher's Note

Combining the complete text of a classic novel or drama with a comprehensive study guide, Dover Thrift Study Editions are the most effective way to gain a thorough understanding of the major works of world literature.

The study guide features up-to-date and expert analysis of every chapter or section from the source work. Questions and fully explained answers follow, allowing readers to analyze the material critically. Character lists, author bios, and discussions of the work's historical context are also provided.

Each Dover Thrift Study Edition includes everything a student needs to prepare for homework, discussions, reports, and exams.

Contents

Twelfth Night vii

Study Guide 73

Twelfth Night
Or, What You Will

WILLIAM SHAKESPEARE

Contents

Dramatis Personae x
Act I. 1
    Scene I 1
    Scene II 2
    Scene III. 4
    Scene IV. 8
    Scene V 9
Act II 18
    Scene I 18
    Scene II 19
    Scene III 20
    Scene IV. 25
    Scene V 29
Act III 34
    Scene I 34
    Scene II 39
    Scene III. 41
    Scene IV. 43
Act IV 53
    Scene I 53
    Scene II 55
    Scene III. 58
Act V 60
    Scene I 60

Dramatis Personæ

ORSINO, Duke of Illyria.
SEBASTIAN, brother to Viola.
ANTONIO, a sea captain, friend to Sebastian.
A Sea Captain, friend to Viola.
VALENTINE,⎫
CURIO,   ⎭ gentlemen attending on the Duke.
SIR TOBY BELCH, uncle to Olivia.
SIR ANDREW AGUECHEEK.
MALVOLIO, steward to Olivia.
FABIAN,   ⎫
FESTE, a Clown, ⎭ servants to Olivia.

OLIVIA.
VIOLA.
MARIA, Olivia's woman.

Lords, Priests, Sailors, Officers, Musicians, and other Attendants.

SCENE: *A city in Illyria, and the sea-coast near it*

ACT I

SCENE I. *An apartment in the* DUKE'S *palace.*

Enter DUKE, CURIO, *and other* Lords; Musicians *attending*

DUKE.   If music be the food of love, play on;
      Give me excess of it, that, surfeiting,
      The appetite may sicken, and so die.
      That strain again! it had a dying fall:
      O, it came o'er my ear like the sweet sound,
      That breathes upon a bank of violets,
      Stealing and giving odour!
      Enough; no more:
      'T is not so sweet now as it was before.
      O spirit of love, how quick and fresh art thou!
      That, notwithstanding thy capacity
      Receiveth as the sea, nought enters there,
      Of what validity and pitch soe'er,
      But falls into abatement and low price,
      Even in a minute! so full of shapes is fancy,
      That it alone is high fantastical.
CUR.   Will you go hunt, my lord?
DUKE.   What, Curio?
CUR.   The hart.
DUKE.   Why, so I do, the noblest that I have:
      O, when mine eyes did see Olivia first,
      Methought she purged the air of pestilence!
      That instant was I turn'd into a hart;
      And my desires, like fell and cruel hounds,
      E'er since pursue me.

Enter VALENTINE

                  How now! what news from her?

1

VAL.   So please my lord, I might not be admitted;
        But from her handmaid do return this answer:
        The element[1] itself, till seven years' heat,
        Shall not behold her face at ample view;
        But, like a cloistress, she will veiled walk
        And water once a day her chamber round
        With eye-offending brine: all this to season
        A brother's dead love, which she would keep fresh
        And lasting in her sad remembrance.
DUKE.   O, she that hath a heart of that fine frame
        To pay this debt of love but to a brother,
        How will she love, when the rich golden shaft
        Hath kill'd the flock of all affections else
        That live in her; when liver, brain and heart,
        These sovereign thrones, are all supplied, and fill'd
        Her sweet perfections with one self king!
        Away before me to sweet beds of flowers:
        Love-thoughts lie rich when canopied with bowers.   [*Exeunt.*]

SCENE II. *The sea-coast.*

Enter VIOLA, *a* Captain, *and* Sailors

VIO.   What country, friends, is this?
CAP.   This is Illyria, lady.
VIO.   And what should I do in Illyria?
        My brother he is in Elysium.
        Perchance he is not drown'd: what think you, sailors?
CAP.   It is perchance that you yourself were saved.
VIO.   O my poor brother! and so perchance may he be.
CAP.   True, madam: and, to comfort you with chance,
        Assure yourself, after our ship did split,
        When you and those poor number saved with you
        Hung on our driving boat, I saw your brother,
        Most provident in peril, bind himself,

_____

1. *element*] sky.

Courage and hope both teaching him the practice,
To a strong mast that lived upon the sea;
Where, like Arion on the dolphin's back,
I saw him hold acquaintance with the waves
So long as I could see.
VIO.   For saying so, there 's gold:
Mine own escape unfoldeth to my hope,
Whereto thy speech serves for authority,
The like of him. Know'st thou this country?
CAP.   Ay, madam, well; for I was bred and born
Not three hours' travel from this very place.
VIO.   Who governs here?
CAP.   A noble Duke,[1] in nature as in name.
VIO.   What is his name?
CAP.   Orsino.
VIO.   Orsino! I have heard my father name him:
He was a bachelor then.
CAP.   And so is now, or was so very late;
For but a month ago I went from hence,
And then 't was fresh in murmur,—as, you know,
What great ones do the less will prattle of,—
That he did seek the love of fair Olivia.
VIO.   What 's she?
CAP.   A virtuous maid, the daughter of a count
That died some twelvemonth since; then leaving her
In the protection of his son, her brother,
Who shortly also died: for whose dear love,
They say, she hath abjured the company
And sight of men.
VIO.   O that I served that lady,
And might not be delivered to the world,
Till I had made mine own occasion mellow,
What my estate is![2]
CAP.   That were hard to compass;
Because she will admit no kind of suit,
No, not the Duke's.
VIO.   There is a fair behaviour in thee, captain;

_____

1. *Duke*] Orsino is subsequently spoken of merely as "Count."
2. *O...is!*] Viola wishes it were possible to keep her name and rank a secret until she chooses to make it known.

And though that nature with a beauteous wall
Doth oft close in pollution, yet of thee
I will believe thou hast a mind that suits
With this thy fair and outward character.
I prithee, and I 'll pay thee bounteously,
Conceal me what I am, and be my aid
For such disguise as haply shall become
The form of my intent. I 'll serve this Duke:
Thou shalt present me as an eunuch to him:
It may be worth thy pains; for I can sing,
And speak to him in many sorts of music,
That will allow me very worth his service.
What else may hap to time I will commit;
Only shape thou thy silence to my wit.

CAP.   Be you his eunuch, and your mute I 'll be:
When my tongue blabs, then let mine eyes not see.

VIO.   I thank thee: lead me on.   [*Exeunt.*]

SCENE III. OLIVIA'S *house.*

Enter SIR TOBY BELCH *and* MARIA

SIR TO.   What a plague means my niece, to take the death of her
brother thus? I am sure care 's an enemy to life.

MAR.   By my troth, Sir Toby, you must come in earlier o' nights: your
cousin, my lady, takes great exceptions to your ill hours.

SIR TO.   Why, let her except, before excepted.

MAR.   Ay, but you must confine yourself within the modest limits of
order.

SIR TO.   Confine! I 'll confine myself no finer than I am: these clothes
are good enough to drink in; and so be these boots too: an they be
not, let them hang themselves in their own straps.

MAR.   That quaffing and drinking will undoe you: I heard my lady
talk of it yesterday; and of a foolish knight that you brought in one
night here to be her wooer.

SIR TO.   Who, Sir Andrew Aguecheek?

MAR.   Ay, he.

SIR TO.   He 's as tall a man as any 's in Illyria.

MAR.   What 's that to the purpose?

SIR TO.   Why, he has three thousand ducats a year.

MAR.   Ay, but he 'll have but a year in all these ducats: he 's a very fool and a prodigal.

SIR TO.   Fie, that you 'll say so! he plays o' the viol-de-gamboys, and speaks three or four languages word for word without book, and hath all the good gifts of nature.

MAR.   He hath indeed, almost natural: for besides that he 's a fool, he 's a great quarreller; and but that he hath the gift of a coward to allay the gust he hath in quarrelling, 't is thought among the prudent he would quickly have the gift of a grave.

SIR TO.   By this hand, they are scoundrels and substractors that say so of him. Who are they?

MAR.   They that add, moreover, he 's drunk nightly in your company.

SIR TO.   With drinking healths to my niece: I 'll drink to her as long as there is a passage in my throat and drink in Illyria: he 's a coward and a coystrill[1] that will not drink to my niece till his brains turn o' the toe like a parish-top.[2] What, wench! Castiliano vulgo;[3] for here comes Sir Andrew Agueface.

Enter SIR ANDREW AGUECHEEK

SIR AND.   Sir Toby Belch! how now, Sir Toby Belch!

SIR TO.   Sweet Sir Andrew!

SIR AND.   Bless you, fair shrew.

MAR.   And you too, sir.

SIR TO.   Accost, Sir Andrew, accost.

SIR AND.   What 's that?

SIR TO.   My niece's chambermaid.

SIR AND.   Good Mistress Accost, I desire better acquaintance.

MAR.   My name is Mary, sir.

SIR AND.   Good Mistress Mary Accost, —

SIR TO.   You mistake, knight: "accost" is front her, board her, woo her, assail her.

SIR AND.   By my troth, I would not undertake her in this company. Is that the meaning of "accost"?

---

1. *coystrill*] a common term of contempt, meaning "a base fellow."
2. *parish-top*] A large top provided by the parochial authorities in Shakespeare's day for boys to play with.
3. *Castiliano vulgo*] literally, the Spanish for "Castilian people."

MAR. Fare you well, gentlemen.

SIR TO. An thou let part so, Sir Andrew, would thou mightst never draw sword again.

SIR AND. An you part so, mistress, I would I might never draw sword again. Fair lady, do you think you have fools in hand?

MAR. Sir, I have not you by the hand.

SIR AND. Marry, but you shall have; and here 's my hand.

MAR. Now, sir, "thought is free": I pray you, bring your hand to the buttery-bar⁴ and let it drink.

SIR AND. Wherefore, sweet-heart? what 's your metaphor?

MAR. It 's dry,⁵ sir.

SIR AND. Why, I think so: I am not such an ass but I can keep my hand dry. But what 's your jest?

MAR. A dry jest,⁶ sir.

SIR AND. Are you full of them?

MAR. Ay, sir, I have them at my fingers' ends: marry, now I let go your hand, I am barren.⁷ [*Exit.*]

SIR TO. O knight, thou lackest a cup of canary:⁸ when did I see thee so put down?

SIR AND. Never in your life, I think; unless you see canary put me down. Methinks sometimes I have no more wit than a Christian or an ordinary man has: but I am a great eater of beef and I believe that does harm to my wit.

SIR TO. No question.

SIR AND. An I thought that, I 'ld forswear it. I 'll ride home to-morrow, Sir Toby.

SIR TO. Pourquoi, my dear knight?

SIR AND. What is "pourquoi"? do or not do? I would I had bestowed that time in the tongues⁹ that I have in fencing, dancing and bear-baiting: O, had I but followed the arts!

SIR TO. Then had'st thou had an excellent head of hair.

SIR AND. Why, would that have mended my hair?

---

4. *buttery-bar*] a room where provisions are stored.

5. *It 's dry*] A dry hand was commonly held to be a sign of indifference to love, as well as of debility and old age. A moist hand was commonly taken to be the sign of an amorous disposition.

6. *A dry jest*] An insipid jest.

7. *barren*] dull, witless, tedious.

8. *canary*] a sweet wine from the Canary Islands.

9. *in the tongues*] studying languages; "tongues" was often written and commonly pronounced as "tongs," and Sir Toby's retort about Sir Andrew's "head of hair" obviously shows that a pun on "tongs" in the sense of curling irons was intended.

SIR TO.   Past question; for thou seest it will not curl by nature.

SIR AND.   But it becomes me well enough, does 't not?

SIR TO.   Excellent; it hangs like flax on a distaff; and I hope to see a housewife take thee between her legs and spin it off.

SIR AND.   Faith, I 'll home to-morrow, Sir Toby: your niece will not be seen; or if she be, it 's four to one she 'll none of me: the count himself here hard by woos her.

SIR TO.   She 'll none o' the count: she 'll not match above her degree, neither in estate, years, nor wit; I have heard her swear 't. Tut, there 's life in 't, man.

SIR AND.   I 'll stay a month longer. I am a fellow o' the strangest mind i' the world; I delight in masques and revels sometimes altogether.

SIR TO.   Art thou good at these kickshawses,[10] knight?

SIR AND.   As any man in Illyria, whatsoever he be, under the degree of my betters; and yet I will not compare with an old man.

SIR TO.   What is thy excellence in a galliard, knight?

SIR AND.   Faith, I can cut a caper.[11]

SIR TO.   And I can cut the mutton to 't.

SIR AND.   And I think I have the back-trick simply as strong as any man in Illyria.

SIR TO.   Wherefore are these things hid? wherefore have these gifts a curtain before 'em? are they like to take dust, like Mistress Mall's picture? why dost thou not go to church in a galliard and come home in a coranto?[12] My very walk should be a jig; I would not so much as make water but in a sink-a-pace.[13] What dost thou mean? Is it a world to hide virtues in? I did think, by the excellent constitution of thy leg, it was formed under the star of a galliard.

SIR AND.   Ay, 't is strong, and it does indifferent well in a flame-coloured stock. Shall we set about some revels?

SIR TO.   What shall we do else? were we not born under Taurus?

SIR AND.   Taurus! That 's sides and heart.

SIR TO.   No, sir; it is legs and thighs.[14] Let me see thee caper: ha! higher: ha, ha! excellent!   [Exeunt.]

---

10. *kickshawses*] toys, trifles.

11. *galliard . . . caper*] lively dances.

12. *coranto*] another lively dance.

13. *sink-a-pace*] a phonetic spelling of "cinque pace," a lively dance.

14. *Taurus . . . thighs*] Astrology assumed that each part of the body was under the control of one or other signs of the zodiac. But both Sir Andrew and Sir Toby are in error in their reference to Taurus, who, according to the authorities, controls neither the "sides and hearts" nor the "legs and thighs," but the neck and throat.

SCENE IV. *The* DUKE'S *palace.*

Enter VALENTINE, *and* VIOLA *in man's attire*

VAL.   If the Duke continue these favours towards you, Cesario,[1] you
    are like to be much advanced: he hath known you but three days,
    and already you are no stranger.
VIO.   You either fear his humour or my negligence, that you call in
    question the continuance of his love: is he constant, sir, in his
    favours?
VAL.   No, believe me.
VIO.   I thank you. Here comes the count.[2]

Enter DUKE, CURIO, *and* Attendants

DUKE.   Who saw Cesario, ho?
VIO.   On your attendance, my lord; here.
DUKE.   Stand you a while aloof. Cesario,
    Thou know'st no less but all; I have unclasp'd
    To thee the book even of my secret soul:
    Therefore, good youth, address thy gait unto her;
    Be not denied access, stand at her doors,
    And tell them, there thy fixed foot shall grow
    Till thou have audience.
VIO.   Sure, my noble lord,
    If she be so abandon'd to her sorrow
    As it is spoke, she never will admit me.
DUKE.   Be clamorous and leap all civil bounds
    Rather than make unprofited return.
VIO.   Say I do speak with her, my lord, what then?
DUKE.   O, then unfold the passion of my love,
    Surprise her with discourse of my dear faith:
    It shall become thee well to act my woes;
    She will attend it better in thy youth
    Than in a nuncio's[3] of more grave aspect.

---

1. *Cesario*] Viola's male alias.
2. *the count*] In the stage directions throughout the play, Orsino is called "Duke," and is
   so spoken of at I, ii, 25. But everywhere else in the text he is referred to as "the count."
3. *nuncio's*] messenger's.

VIO.   I think not so, my lord.
DUKE.   Dear lad, believe it;
    For they shall yet belie thy happy years,
    That say thou art a man: Diana's lip
    Is not more smooth and rubious;[4] thy small pipe
    Is as the maiden's organ, shrill and sound;
    And all is semblative[5] a woman's part.
    I know thy constellation is right apt
    For this affair. Some four or five attend him;
    All, if you will; for I myself am best
    When least in company. Prosper well in this,
    And thou shalt live as freely as thy lord,
    To call his fortunes thine.
VIO.   I 'll do my best
    To woo your lady: [*Aside*] yet, a barful[6] strife!
    Whoe'er I woo, myself would be his wife.   [*Exeunt.*]

SCENE V. OLIVIA'S *house.*

Enter MARIA *and* Clown

MAR.   Nay, either tell me where thou hast been, or I will not open my
    lips so wide as a bristle may enter in way of thy excuse: my lady
    will hang thee for thy absence.
CLO.   Let her hang me: he that is well hanged in this world needs to
    fear no colours.[1]
MAR.   Make that good.
CLO.   He shall see none to fear.
MAR.   A good lenten[2] answer: I can tell thee where that saying was
    born, of "I fear no colours."
CLO.   Where, good Mistress Mary?

---

4. *rubious*] apparently a once-used word; formed from "ruby."
5. *semblative*] like or similar to.
6. *barful*] full of obstacles.

---

1. *fear no colours*] fear no enemies; "colours" were ensigns or standards, which would have
    been displayed during battles.
2. *lenten*] scanty, spare.

MAR. In the wars; and that may you be bold to say in your foolery.
CLO. Well, God give them wisdom that have it; and those that are fools, let them use their talents.
MAR. Yet you will be hanged for being so long absent; or, to be turned away, is not that as good as a hanging to you?
CLO. Many a good hanging prevents a bad marriage; and, for turning away, let summer bear it out.[3]
MAR. You are resolute, then?
CLO. Not so, neither; but I am resolved on two points.
MAR. That if one break, the other will hold; or, if both break, your gaskins fall.[4]
CLO. Apt, in good faith; very apt. Well, go thy way; if Sir Toby would leave drinking, thou wert as witty a piece of Eve's flesh as any in Illyria.
MAR. Peace, you rogue, no more o' that. Here comes my lady: make your excuse wisely, you were best.   [*Exit.*]
CLO. Wit, an 't be thy will, put me into good fooling! Those wits, that think they have thee, do very oft prove fools; and I, that am sure I lack thee, may pass for a wise man: for what says Quinapalus?[5] "Better a witty fool than a foolish wit."

Enter LADY OLIVIA *with* MALVOLIO

God bless thee, lady!
OLI. Take the fool away.
CLO. Do you not hear, fellows? Take away the lady.
OLI. Go to, you 're a dry fool; I 'll no more of you: besides, you grow dishonest.
CLO. Two faults, madonna, that drink and good counsel will amend: for give the dry fool drink, then is the fool not dry: bid the dishonest man mend himself; if he mend, he is no longer dishonest; if he cannot, let the botcher mend him. Any thing that 's mended is but patched: virtue that transgresses is but patched with sin; and sin that amends is but patched with virtue. If that this simple syllogism will serve, so; if it will not, what remedy? As there is no true cuckold but calamity, so beauty 's a flower. The lady bade take away the fool; therefore, I say again, take her away.

---

3. *for turning . . . out*] If I am threatened with dismissal, let us wait for next season,—next summer,—and see if the threat take effect, i.e., wait awhile and see.
4. *points . . . fall*] a "point" was a metal hook or tag, which attaches the gaskins, i.e., breeches or hose, to the doublet.
5. *Quinapalus*] An apocryphal philosopher invented for the occasion.

OLI.   Sir, I bade them take away you.

CLO.   Misprision[6] in the highest degree! Lady, cucullus non facit monachum;[7] that 's as much to say as I wear not motley in my brain. Good madonna, give me leave to prove you a fool.

OLI.   Can you do it?

CLO.   Dexteriously,[8] good madonna.

OLI.   Make your proof.

CLO.   I must catechize you for it, madonna: good my mouse of virtue, answer me.

OLI.   Well, sir, for want of other idleness, I 'll bide your proof.

CLO.   Good madonna, why mournest thou?

OLI.   Good fool, for my brother's death.

CLO.   I think his soul is in hell, madonna.

OLI.   I know his soul is in heaven, fool.

CLO.   The more fool, madonna, to mourn for your brother's soul being in heaven. Take away the fool, gentlemen.

OLI.   What think you of this fool, Malvolio? doth he not mend?

MAL.   Yes, and shall do till the pangs of death shake him: infirmity, that decays the wise, doth ever make the better fool.

CLO.   God send you, sir, a speedy infirmity, for the better increasing your folly! Sir Toby will be sworn that I am no fox; but he will not pass his word for two pence that you are no fool.

OLI.   How say you to that, Malvolio?

MAL.   I marvel your ladyship takes delight in such a barren rascal: I saw him put down the other day with an ordinary fool that has no more brain than a stone. Look you now, he 's out of his guard already; unless you laugh and minister occasion to him, he is gagged. I protest, I take these wise men, that crow so at these set kind of fools, no better than the fools' zanies.[9]

OLI.   O, you are sick of self-love, Malvolio, and taste with a distempered appetite. To be generous, guiltless and of free disposition, is to take those things for bird-bolts[10] that you deem cannon-bullets: there is no slander in an allowed fool, though he do nothing but

---

6. *Misprision*] Legally the term "misprision," which literally means "contempt," was applied to evil speaking of the sovereign.

7. *cucullus . . . monachum*] "The cowl does not make the monk," a proverb in vogue throughout Europe.

8. *Dexteriously*] Dexterously.

9. *zanies*] a subordinate buffoon whose duty was to make awkward attempts at mimicking the tricks of the professional clown.

10. *bird-bolts*] short arrows with broad flat ends, used to kill birds without piercing them.

rail; nor no railing in a known discreet man, though he do nothing but reprove.

CLO.   Now Mercury endue thee with leasing,[11] for thou speakest well
of fools!

Re-enter MARIA

MAR.   Madam, there is at the gate a young gentleman much desires to
speak with you.

OLI.   From the Count Orsino, is it?

MAR.   I know not, madam: 't is a fair young man, and well attended.

OLI.   Who of my people hold him in delay?

MAR.   Sir Toby, madam, your kinsman.

OLI.   Fetch him off, I pray you; he speaks nothing but madman: fie on
him! [*Exit* MARIA.] Go you, Malvolio: if it be a suit from the
count, I am sick, or not at home; what you will, to dismiss it. [*Exit*
MALVOLIO.] Now you see, sir, how your fooling grows old, and
people dislike it.

CLO.   Thou hast spoke for us, madonna, as if thy eldest son should be
a fool; whose skull Jove cram with brains! for, — here he comes, —
one of thy kin has a most weak pia mater.[12]

Enter SIR TOBY

OLI.   By mine honour, half drunk. What is he at the gate, cousin?

SIR TO.   A gentleman.

OLI.   A gentleman! what gentleman?

SIR TO.   'T is a gentleman here — a plague o' these pickle-herring![13]
How now, sot!

CLO.   Good Sir Toby!

OLI.   Cousin, cousin, how have you come so early by this lethargy?

SIR TO.   Lechery! I defy lechery. There 's one at the gate.

OLI.   Ay, marry, what is he?

SIR TO.   Let him be the devil, an he will, I care not: give me faith, say
I. Well, it 's all one.   [*Exit.*]

OLI.   What 's a drunken man like, fool?

CLO.   Like a drowned man, a fool and a mad man: one draught above

---

11. *Mercury . . . leasing*] May the god of cheats or liars endow thee, to thy profit, with the
gift of lying.

12. *pia mater*] the membrane that covers the brain; the term was used for the brain itself.

13. *pickle-herring*] the favourite relish for drunkards.

heat[14] makes him a fool; the second mads him; and a third drowns
him.

OLI.   Go thou and seek the crowner,[15] and let him sit o' my coz; for he
's in the third degree of drink, he 's drowned: go look after him.

CLO.   He is but mad yet, madonna; and the fool shall look to the madman.   [*Exit.*]

Re-enter MALVOLIO

MAL.   Madam, yond young fellow swears he will speak with you. I told
him you were sick; he takes on him to understand so much, and
therefore comes to speak with you. I told him you were asleep; he
seems to have a foreknowledge of that too, and therefore comes to
speak with you. What is to be said to him, lady? he 's fortified
against any denial.

OLI.   Tell him he shall not speak with me.

MAL.   Has been told so; and he says, he 'll stand at your door like a
sheriff's post,[16] and be the supporter to a bench, but he 'll speak
with you.

OLI.   What kind o' man is he?

MAL.   Why, of mankind.

OLI.   What manner of man?

MAL.   Of very ill manner; he 'll speak with you, will you or no.

OLI.   Of what personage and years is he?

MAL.   Not yet old enough for a man, nor young enough for a boy; as
a squash is before 't is a peascod, or a codling[17] when 't is almost
an apple: 't is with him in standing water,[18] between boy and man.
He is very well-favoured and he speaks very shrewishly; one would
think his mother's milk were scarce out of him.

OLI.   Let him approach: call in my gentlewoman.

MAL.   Gentlewoman, my lady calls.   [*Exit.*]

Re-enter MARIA

OLI.   Give me my veil: come, throw it o'er my face. We 'll once more
hear Orsino's embassy.

---

14. *above heat*] above ordinary strength.
15. *crowner*] coroner.
16. *sheriff's post*] a post, often carved with elaborate ornament, which stood before the
door of the house occupied by a city mayor and sheriff.
17. *squash . . . codling*] terms respectively for an unripe peascod and an unripe apple.
18. *in standing water*] just at the turn of the tide, in the condition of stationary water that
neither ebbs nor flows.

Enter VIOLA, *and* Attendants

VIO. The honourable lady of the house, which is she?

OLI. Speak to me; I shall answer for her. Your will?

VIO. Most radiant, exquisite and unmatchable beauty,—I pray you, tell me if this be the lady of the house, for I never saw her: I would be loath to cast away my speech, for besides that it is excellently well penned, I have taken great pains to con it. Good beauties, let me sustain no scorn; I am very comptible,[19] even to the least sinister usage.

OLI. Whence came you, sir?

VIO. I can say little more than I have studied, and that question 's out of my part. Good gentle one, give me modest assurance if you be the lady of the house, that I may proceed in my speech.

OLI. Are you a comedian?

VIO. No, my profound heart: and yet, by the very fangs of malice I swear, I am not that I play. Are you the lady of the house?

OLI. If I do not usurp myself, I am.

VIO. Most certain, if you are she, you do usurp yourself; for what is yours to bestow is not yours to reserve. But this is from my commission: I will on with my speech in your praise, and then show you the heart of my message.

OLI. Come to what is important in 't: I forgive you the praise.

VIO. Alas, I took great pains to study it, and 't is poetical.

OLI. It is the more like to be feigned: I pray you, keep it in. I heard you were saucy at my gates, and allowed your approach rather to wonder at you than to hear you. If you be not mad, be gone; if you have reason, be brief: 't is not that time of moon with me to make one in so skipping a dialogue.[20]

MAR. Will you hoist sail, sir? here lies your way.

VIO. No, good swabber;[21] I am to hull[22] here a little longer. Some mollification for your giant,[23] sweet lady. Tell me your mind: I am a messenger.

---

19. *comptible*] sensitive.

20. *'t is . . . dialogue*] the waning and waxing of the moon served as images of change; the sense here is that Olivia is in no mood or humor to entertain any flighty or thoughtless (skipping) exchange with Viola/Cassio.

21. *swabber*] one who mops the ship's deck at sea.

22. *hull*] drift with the sails furled.

23. *giant*] an ironical reference to Maria, who, as implied elsewhere in the play, is small in size.

OLI.   Sure, you have some hideous matter to deliver, when the courtesy of it is so fearful. Speak your office.

VIO.   It alone concerns your ear. I bring no overture of war, no taxa-
tion of homage: I hold the olive in my hand; my words are as full
of peace as matter.

OLI.   Yet you began rudely. What are you? what would you?

VIO.   The rudeness that hath appeared in me have I learned from my
entertainment. What I am, and what I would, are as secret as
maidenhead; to your ears, divinity, to any other's, profanation.

OLI.   Give us the place alone: we will hear this divinity. [*Exeunt*
MARIA *and* Attendants.] Now, sir, what is your text?

VIO.   Most sweet lady,—

OLI.   A comfortable doctrine, and much may be said of it. Where lies
your text?

VIO.   In Orsino's bosom.

OLI.   In his bosom! In what chapter of his bosom?

VIO.   To answer by the method, in the first of his heart.

OLI.   O, I have read it: it is heresy. Have you no more to say?

VIO.   Good madam, let me see your face.

OLI.   Have you any commission from your lord to negotiate with my
face? You are now out of your text: but we will draw the curtain
and show you the picture. Look you, sir, such a one I was this present: is 't not well done?   [*Unveiling.*]

VIO.   Excellently done, if God did all.

OLI.   'T is in grain,[24] sir; 't will endure wind and weather.

VIO.   'T is beauty truly blent, whose red and white
Nature's own sweet and cunning hand laid on:
Lady, you are the cruell'st she alive,
If you will lead these graces to the grave
And leave the world no copy.

OLI.   O, sir, I will not be so hard-hearted; I will give out divers sched-
ules of my beauty: it shall be inventoried, and every particle and
utensil labelled to my will: as, item, two lips, indifferent red; item,
two grey eyes, with lids to them; item, one neck, one chin, and so
forth. Were you sent hither to praise me?

VIO.   I see you what you are, you are too proud;
But, if you were the devil, you are fair.
My lord and master loves you: O, such love
Could be but recompensed, though you were crown'd

---

24. *in grain*] of a fast dye that will not wash out.

The nonpareil of beauty!
OLI.   How does he love me?
VIO.   With adorations, fertile tears,
With groans that thunder love, with sighs of fire.
OLI.   Your lord does know my mind; I cannot love him:
Yet I suppose him virtuous, know him noble,
Of great estate, of fresh and stainless youth;
In voices well divulged,[25] free, learn'd and valiant;
And in dimension and the shape of nature
A gracious person; but yet I cannot love him;
He might have took his answer long ago.
VIO.   If I did love you in my master's flame,
With such a suffering, such a deadly life,
In your denial I would find no sense;
I would not understand it.
OLI.   Why, what would you?
VIO.   Make me a willow cabin at your gate,
And call upon my soul within the house;
Write loyal cantons of contemned love
And sing them loud even in the dead of night;
Halloo your name to the reverberate hills,
And make the babbling gossip of the air
Cry out "Olivia!" O, you should not rest
Between the elements of air and earth,
But you should pity me!
OLI.   You might do much.
What is your parentage?
VIO.   Above my fortunes, yet my state is well:
I am a gentleman.
OLI.   Get you to your lord;
I cannot love him: let him send no more;
Unless, perchance, you come to me again,
To tell me how he takes it. Fare you well:
I thank you for your pains: spend this for me.
VIO.   I am no fee'd post,[26] lady; keep your purse:
My master, not myself, lacks recompense.
Love make his heart of flint that you shall love;
And let your fervour, like my master's, be

25. *well divulged*] well spoken of by the world.
26. *fee'd post*] hired messenger.

     Placed in contempt! Farewell, fair cruelty.   [*Exit.*]
OLI.   "What is your parentage?"
     "Above my fortunes, yet my state is well:
     I am a gentleman." I 'll be sworn thou art;
     Thy tongue, thy face, thy limbs, actions, and spirit,
     Do give thee five-fold blazon:[27] not too fast: soft, soft!
     Unless the master were the man. How now!
     Even so quickly may one catch the plague?
     Methinks I feel this youth's perfections
     With an invisible and subtle stealth
     To creep in at mine eyes. Well, let it be.
     What ho, Malvolio!

Re-enter MALVOLIO

MAL.   Here, madam, at your service.
OLI.   Run after that same peevish messenger,
     The county's man: he left this ring behind him,
     Would I or not: tell him I 'll none of it.
     Desire him not to flatter with his lord,
     Nor hold him up with hopes; I am not for him:
     If that the youth will come this way to-morrow,
     I 'll give him reasons for 't: hie thee, Malvolio.
MAL.   Madam, I will.   [*Exit.*]
OLI.   I do I know not what, and fear to find
     Mine eye too great a flatterer for my mind.
     Fate, show thy force: ourselves we do not owe;
     What is decreed must be, and be this so.   [*Exit.*]

---

27. *blazon*] coat of arms.

ACT II

SCENE I. *The sea-coast.*

Enter ANTONIO *and* SEBASTIAN

ANT.   Will you stay no longer? nor will you not that I go with you?

SEB.   By your patience, no. My stars shine darkly over me: the malignancy of my fate might perhaps distemper yours; therefore I shall crave of you your leave that I may bear my evils alone: it were a bad recompense for your love, to lay any of them on you.

ANT.   Let me yet know of you whither you are bound.

SEB.   No, sooth, sir: my determinate voyage is mere extravagancy.[1] But I perceive in you so excellent a touch of modesty, that you will not extort from me what I am willing to keep in; therefore it charges me in manners the rather to express myself. You must know of me then, Antonio, my name is Sebastian, which I called Roderigo. My father was that Sebastian of Messaline, whom I know you have heard of. He left behind him myself and a sister, both born in an hour: if the heavens had been pleased, would we had so ended! but you, sir, altered that; for some hour before you took me from the breach of the sea was my sister drowned.

ANT.   Alas the day!

SEB.   A lady, sir, though it was said she much resembled me, was yet of many accounted beautiful: but, though I could not with such estimable wonder overfar believe that, yet thus far I will boldly publish her; she bore a mind that envy could not but call fair. She is drowned already, sir, with salt water, though I seem to drown her remembrance again with more.

ANT.   Pardon me, sir, your bad entertainment.

SEB.   O good Antonio, forgive me your trouble.

ANT.   If you will not murder me for my love, let me be your servant.

SEB.   If you will not undo what you have done, that is, kill him whom you have recovered, desire it not. Fare ye well at once: my bosom is full of kindness, and I am yet so near the manners of my moth-

---

1. *my determinate . . . extravagancy*] The voyage I have resolved upon is mere vagrancy, mere roaming.

er, that upon the least occasion more mine eyes will tell tales of
me. I am bound to the Count Orsino's court: farewell.   [*Exit.*]
ANT.   The gentleness of all the gods go with thee!
I have many enemies in Orsino's court,
Else would I very shortly see thee there.
But, come what may, I do adore thee so,
That danger shall seem sport, and I will go.   [*Exit.*]

SCENE II. *A street.*

Enter VIOLA, MALVOLIO *following*

MAL.   Were not you even now with the Countess Olivia?

VIO.   Even now, sir; on a moderate pace I have since arrived but hither.

MAL.   She returns this ring to you, sir: you might have saved me my
pains, to have taken it away yourself. She adds, moreover, that you
should put your lord into a desperate assurance she will none of
him: and one thing more, that you be never so hardy to come
again in his affairs, unless it be to report your lord's taking of this.
Receive it so.

VIO.   She took the ring of me: I 'll none of it.

MAL.   Come, sir, you peevishly threw it to her; and her will is, it
should be so returned: if it be worth stooping for, there it lies in
your eye; if not, be it his that finds it.   [*Exit.*]

VIO.   I left no ring with her: what means this lady?
Fortune forbid my outside have not charm'd her!
She made good view of me; indeed, so much,
That methought her eyes had lost her tongue,
For she did speak in starts distractedly.
She loves me, sure; the cunning of her passion
Invites me in this churlish messenger.
None of my lord's ring! why, he sent her none.
I am the man: if it be so, as 't is,
Poor lady, she were better love a dream.
Disguise, I see, thou art a wickedness,

Wherein the pregnant enemy[1] does much.
How easy is it for the proper-false
In women's waxen hearts to set their forms!
Alas, our frailty is the cause, not we!
For such as we are made of, such we be.
How will this fadge?[2] my master loves her dearly;
And I, poor monster, fond as much on him;
And she, mistaken, seems to dote on me.
What will become of this? As I am man,
My state is desperate for my master's love;
As I am woman,—now alas the day!—
What thriftless sighs shall poor Olivia breathe!
O time! thou must untangle this, not I;
It is too hard a knot for me to untie!   [*Exit.*]

SCENE III. OLIVIA'S *house.*

Enter SIR TOBY *and* SIR ANDREW

SIR TO.   Approach, Sir Andrew: not to be a-bed after midnight is to be up betimes; and "diluculo surgere,"[1] thou know'st,—

SIR AND.   Nay, by my troth, I know not: but I know, to be up late is to be up late.

SIR TO.   A false conclusion: I hate it as an unfilled can. To be up after midnight and to go to bed then, is early: so that to go to bed after midnight is to go to bed betimes. Does not our life consist of the four elements?

SIR AND.   Faith, so they say; but I think it rather consists of eating and drinking.

SIR TO.   Thou 'rt a scholar; let us therefore eat and drink. Marian, I say! a stoup of wine!

Enter Clown

---

1. *the pregnant enemy*] the alert enemy of mankind, i.e., the devil.
2. *fadge*] turn out.

---

1. "*diluculo surgere*"] sc. saluberrimum est, "To rise at dawn is very healthy."

SIR AND.   Here comes the fool, i' faith.

CLO.   How now, my hearts! did you never see the picture of "we three"?[2]

SIR TO.   Welcome, ass. Now let 's have a catch.[3]

SIR AND.   By my troth, the fool has an excellent breast. I had rather than forty shillings I had such a leg, and so sweet a breath to sing, as the fool has. In sooth, thou wast in very gracious fooling last night, when thou spokest of Pigrogromitus, of the Vapians passing the equinoctial of Queubus:[4] 't was very good, i' faith. I sent thee sixpence for thy leman:[5] hadst it?

CLO.   I did impeticos thy gratillity; for Malvolio's nose is no whip-stock: my lady has a white hand, and the Myrmidons are no bot-tle-ale houses.[6]

SIR AND.   Excellent! why, this is the best fooling, when all is done. Now, a song.

SIR TO.   Come on; there is sixpence for you: let 's have a song.

SIR AND.   There 's a testril[7] of me too: if one knight give a—

CLO.   Would you have a love-song, or a song of good life?

SIR TO.   A love-song, a love-song.

SIR AND.   Ay, ay: I care not for good life.

CLO.   [Sings]

>   O mistress mine, where are you roaming?
>   O, stay and hear; your true love's coming,
>   That can sing both high and low:
>   Trip no further, pretty sweeting;
>   Journeys end in lovers meeting,
>   Every wise man's son doth know.

SIR AND.   Excellent good, i' faith.

SIR TO.   Good, good.

---

2. *picture of "we three"*] a common ale-house sign on which was painted the heads of two fools, or two asses, with the legend "We three logger-heads be." The spectator makes up the trio.

3. *a catch*] a song sung in succession, i.e. a round.

4. *Pigrogromitus . . . Queubus*] proper names invented for the occasion.

5. *leman*] lover.

6. *I did impeticos . . . houses*] The clown talks nonsense to something of this effect: "I impocketed thy diminutive gratuity (or I gave it to my petticoat companion). Malvolio's inquisitive nose may smell out our sins, but cannot punish them. My sweetheart is a lady of refinement, and the myrmidons, the humbler retainers of a noble household, are not of the vulgar and coarse character attaching to pot-houses."

7. *testril*] sixpence.

CLO.   [*Sings*]

> What is love? 't is not hereafter;
> Present mirth hath present laughter;
>   What 's to come is still unsure:
> In delay there lies no plenty;
> Then come kiss me, sweet and twenty,
>   Youth 's a stuff will not endure.

SIR AND.   A mellifluous voice, as I am true knight.

SIR TO.   A contagicus breath.

SIR AND.   Very sweet and contagious, i' faith.

SIR TO.   To hear by the nose, it is dulcet in contagion. But shall we make the welkin dance indeed? shall we rouse the night-owl in a catch that will draw three souls out of one weaver?[8] shall we do that?

SIR AND.   An you love me, let 's do 't: I am dog at a catch.

CLO.   By 'r lady, sir, and some dogs will catch well.

SIR AND.   Most certain. Let our catch be, "Thou knave."

CLO.   "Hold thy peace, thou knave," knight? I shall be constrained in 't to call thee knave, knight.

SIR AND.   'T is not the first time I have constrained one to call me knave. Begin, fool: it begins "Hold thy peace."

CLO.   I shall never begin if I hold my peace.

SIR AND.   Good, i' faith. Come, begin.   [*Catch sung.*]

Enter MARIA

MAR.   What a caterwauling do you keep here! If my lady have not called up her steward Malvolio and bid him turn you out of doors, never trust me.

SIR TO.   My lady 's a Cataian,[9] we are politicians, Malvolio 's a Peg-a-Ramsey, and "Three merry men be we."[10] Am not I consanguineous? am I not of her blood? Tillyvally. Lady! [*Sings*] "There dwelt a man in Babylon, lady, lady!"

CLO.   Beshrew me, the knight 's in admirable fooling.

SIR AND.   Ay, he does well enough if he be disposed, and so do I too: he does it with a better grace, but I do it more natural.

SIR TO.   [*Sings*] "O, the twelfth day of December,"—

---

8. *catch . . . weaver*] Weavers were commonly held to be good singers. The "catch that will draw three souls out of one weaver" must have rare powers of enchantment.

9. *a Cataian*] a Chinese person (used as a term of reproach).

10. *Peg-a-Ramsey. . . be we*"] songs.

MAR. For the love o' God, peace!

Enter MALVOLIO

MAL. My masters, are you mad? or what are you? Have you no wit, manners, nor honesty, but to gabble like tinkers at this time of night? Do ye make an ale-house of my lady's house, that ye squeak out your coziers'[11] catches without any mitigation or remorse of voice? Is there no respect of place, persons, nor time in you?

SIR TO. We did keep time, sir, in our catches. Sneck up!

MAL. Sir Toby, I must be round with you. My lady bade me tell you, that, though she harbours you as her kinsman, she 's nothing allied to your disorders. If you can separate yourself and your misdemeanours, you are welcome to the house; if not, an it would please you to take leave of her, she is very willing to bid you farewell.

SIR TO. "Farewell, dear heart, since I must needs be gone."

MAR. Nay, good Sir Toby.

CLO. "His eyes do show his days are almost done."

MAL. Is 't even so?

SIR TO. "But I will never die."

CLO. Sir Toby, there you lie.

MAL. This is much credit to you.

SIR TO. "Shall I bid him go?"

CLO. "What an if you do?"

SIR TO. "Shall I bid him go, and spare not?"

CLO. "O no, no, no, no, you dare not."

SIR TO. Out o' tune, sir: ye lie. Art any more than a steward? Dost thou think, because thou art virtuous, there shall be no more cakes and ale?

CLO. Yes, by Saint Anne, and ginger shall be hot i' the mouth too.

SIR TO. Thou 'rt i' the right. Go, sir, rub your chain[12] with crums. A stoup of wine, Maria!

MAL. Mistress Mary, if you prized my lady's favour at any thing more than contempt, you would not give means for this uncivil rule: she shall know of it, by this hand.   [*Exit.*]

MAR. Go shake your ears.

SIR AND. 'T were as good a deed as to drink when a man 's a-hungry,

---

11. *coziers*'] cobblers'.
12. *rub your chain*] Stewards wore gold chains round their necks in right of their office.

to challenge him the field, and then to break promise with him and make a fool of him.

SIR TO. Do 't, knight: I 'll write thee a challenge; or I 'll deliver thy indignation to him by word of mouth.

MAR. Sweet Sir Toby, be patient for to-night: since the youth of the count's was to-day with my lady, she is much out of quiet. For Monsieur Malvolio, let me alone with him: if I do not gull him into a nayword,[13] and make him a common recreation, do not think I have wit enough to lie straight in my bed: I know I can do it.

SIR TO. Possess us, possess us; tell us something of him.

MAR. Marry, sir, sometimes he is a kind of puritan.

SIR AND. O, if I thought that, I 'ld beat him like a dog!

SIR TO. What, for being a puritan? thy exquisite reason, dear knight?

SIR AND. I have no exquisite reason for 't, but I have reason good enough.

MAR. The devil a puritan that he is, or any thing constantly, but a time-pleaser; an affectioned ass, that cons state without book and utters it by great swarths:[14] the best persuaded of himself, so crammed, as he thinks, with excellencies, that it is his grounds of faith that all that look on him love him; and on that vice in him will my revenge find notable cause to work.

SIR TO. What wilt thou do?

MAR. I will drop in his way some obscure epistles of love; wherein, by the colour of his beard, the shape of his leg, the manner of his gait, the expressure[15] of his eye, forehead, and complexion, he shall find himself most feelingly personated. I can write very like my lady your niece: on a forgotten matter we can hardly make distinction of our hands.

SIR TO. Excellent! I smell a device.

SIR AND. I have 't in my nose too.

SIR TO. He shall think, by the letters that thou wilt drop, that they come from my niece, and that she 's in love with him.

MAR. My purpose is, indeed, a horse of that colour.

SIR AND. And your horse now would make him an ass.

MAR. Ass, I doubt not.

SIR AND. O, 't will be admirable!

---

13. *gull him . . . nayword*] trick him so that he becomes a byword or laughing-stock.

14. *cons . . . swarths*] learns by heart gossip of state affairs and spouts it in great lengths or masses.

15. *expressure*] accurate description.

MAR.   Sport royal, I warrant you: I know my physic will work with
          him. I will plant you two, and let the fool make a third, where he
          shall find the letter: observe his construction of it. For this night,
          to bed, and dream on the event. Farewell.   [*Exit.*]

SIR TO.   Good night, Penthesilea.[16]

SIR AND.   Before me, she 's a good wench.

SIR TO.   She 's a beagle, true-bred, and one that adores me: what o'
          that?

SIR AND.   I was adored once too.

SIR TO.   Let 's to bed, knight. Thou hadst need send for more money.

SIR AND.   If I cannot recover your niece, I am a foul way out.

SIR TO.   Send for money, knight: if thou hast her not i' the end, call
          me cut.[17]

SIR AND.   If I do not, never trust me, take it how you will.

SIR TO.   Come, come, I 'll go burn some sack; 't is too late to go to
          bed now: come, knight; come, knight.   [*Exeunt.*]

SCENE IV. *The* DUKE'S *palace.*

Enter DUKE, VIOLA, CURIO, *and others*

DUKE.   Give me some music. Now, good morrow, friends.
          Now, good Cesario, but that piece of song,
          That old and antique song we heard last night:
          Methought it did relieve my passion much,
          More than light airs and recollected terms[1]
          Of these most brisk and giddy-paced times:
          Come, but one verse.

CUR.   He is not here, so please your lordship, that should sing it.

DUKE.   Who was it?

CUR.   Feste, the jester, my lord; a fool that the lady Olivia's father took
          much delight in. He is about the house.

DUKE.   Seek him out, and play the tune the while.

---

16. *Penthesilea*] Queen of the Amazons (another ironic reference to Maria's small size).
17. *cut*] a common expression of contempt, "cut" meaning a bobtailed horse.

---

1. *recollected terms*] studied or stilted expressions; phrases lacking spontaneity.

[*Exit* CURIO. *Music plays.*]

Come hither, boy: if ever thou shalt love,
In the sweet pangs of it remember me;
For such as I am all true lovers are,
Unstaid and skittish in all motions else,
Save in the constant image of the creature
That is beloved. How dost thou like this tune?

VIO. It gives a very echo to the seat
Where Love is throned.

DUKE.   Thou dost speak masterly:
My life upon 't, young though thou art, thine eye
Hath stay'd upon some favour that it loves:
Hath it not, boy?

VIO.   A little, by your favour.

DUKE. What kind of woman is 't?

VIO.   Of your complexion.

DUKE. She is not worth thee, then. What years, i' faith?

VIO. About your years, my lord.

DUKE. Too old, by heaven: let still the woman take
An elder than herself; so wears she to him,
So sways she level in her husband's heart:
For, boy, however we do praise ourselves,
Our fancies are more giddy and unfirm,
More longing, wavering, sooner lost and worn,
Than women's are.

VIO.   I think it well, my lord.

DUKE. Then let thy love be younger than thyself,
Or thy affection cannot hold the bent;
For women are as roses, whose fair flower
Being once display'd, doth fall that very hour.

VIO. And so they are: alas, that they are so;
To die, even when they to perfection grow!

Re-enter CURIO *and* Clown

DUKE. O, fellow, come, the song we had last night.
Mark it, Cesario, it is old and plain;
The spinsters and the knitters in the sun
And the free maids that weave their thread with bones
Do use to chant it: it is silly sooth,
And dallies with the innocence of love,

       Like the old age.[2]

CLO.   Are you ready, sir?

DUKE.   Ay; prithee, sing.   [*Music.*]

SONG

CLO.   Come away, come away, death,
     And in sad cypress[3] let me be laid;
   Fly away, fly away, breath;
     I am slain by a fair cruel maid.
   My shroud of white, stuck all with yew,
       O, prepare it!
   My part of death, no one so true
       Did share it.

   Not a flower, not a flower sweet,
     On my black coffin let there be strown;
   Not a friend, not a friend greet
     My poor corpse, where my bones shall be thrown:
   A thousand thousand sighs to save,
       Lay me, O, where
   Sad true lover never find my grave,
       To weep there!

DUKE.   There 's for thy pains.

CLO.   No pains, sir; I take pleasure in singing, sir.

DUKE.   I 'll pay thy pleasure then.

CLO.   Truly, sir, and pleasure will be paid, one time or another.

DUKE.   Give me now leave to leave thee.

CLO.   Now, the melancholy god protect thee; and the tailor make thy doublet of changeable taffeta, for thy mind is a very opal. I would have men of such constancy put to sea, that their business might be every thing and their intent every where; for that 's it that always makes a good voyage of nothing. Farewell.   [*Exit.*]

DUKE.   Let all the rest give place.   [CURIO *and* Attendants *retire.*]
                              Once more, Cesario,
Get thee to yond same sovereign cruelty:
Tell her, my love, more noble than the world,
Prizes not quantity of dirty lands;
The parts that fortune hath bestow'd upon her,
Tell her, I hold as giddily as fortune;

---

2. *the old age*] times past.
3. *cypress*] coffin of cypress wood.

But 't is that miracle and queen of gems
That nature pranks her in attracts my soul.
VIO.   But if she cannot love you, sir?
DUKE.   I cannot be so answer'd.
VIO.   Sooth, but you must.
Say that some lady, as perhaps there is,
Hath for your love as great a pang of heart
As you have for Olivia: you cannot love her;
You tell her so; must she not then be answer'd?
DUKE.   There is no woman's sides
Can bide the beating of so strong a passion
As love doth give my heart; no woman's heart
So big, to hold so much; they lack retention.[4]
Alas, their love may be call'd appetite,—
No motion of the liver, but the palate,—
That suffer surfeit, cloyment[5] and revolt;
But mine is all as hungry as the sea,
And can digest as much: make no compare
Between that love a woman can bear me
And that I owe Olivia.
VIO.   Ay, but I know,—
DUKE.   What dost thou know?
VIO.   Too well what love women to men may owe:
In faith, they are as true of heart as we.
My father had a daughter loved a man,
As it might be, perhaps, were I a woman,
I should your lordship.
DUKE.   And what 's her history?
VIO.   A blank, my lord. She never told her love,
But let concealment, like a worm i' the bud,
Feed on her damask cheek: she pined in thought;
And with a green and yellow melancholy
She sat like patience on a monument,
Smiling at grief. Was not this love indeed?
We men may say more, swear more: but indeed
Our shows are more than will; for still we prove
Much in our vows, but little in our love.
DUKE.   But died thy sister of her love, my boy?

---

4. *retention*] power of retaining.
5. *cloyment*] satiety.

VIO.   I am all the daughters of my father's house,
       And all the brothers too: and yet I know not.
       Sir, shall I to this lady?
DUKE.   Ay, that 's the theme.
       To her in haste; give her this jewel; say,
       My love can give no place, bide no denay.   [*Exeunt.*]

SCENE V. OLIVIA'S *garden.*

Enter SIR TOBY, SIR ANDREW, *and* FABIAN

SIR TO.   Come thy ways, Signior Fabian.
FAB.   Nay, I 'll come: if I lose a scruple of this sport, let me be boiled
       to death with melancholy.
SIR TO.   Wouldst thou not be glad to have the niggardly rascally
       sheep-biter¹ come by some notable shame?
FAB.   I would exult, man: you know, he brought me out o' favour with
       my lady about a bear-baiting here.
SIR TO.   To anger him we 'll have the bear again; and we will fool him
       black and blue: shall we not, Sir Andrew?
SIR AND.   An we do not, it is pity of our lives.
SIR TO.   Here comes the little villain.

Enter MARIA

       How now, my metal of India!²
MAR.   Get ye all three into the box-tree: Malvolio's coming down this
       walk: he has been yonder i' the sun practising behaviour to his
       own shadow this half hour: observe him, for the love of mockery;
       for I know this letter will make a contemplative idiot of him.
       Close, in the name of jesting! Lie thou there [*throws down a let-
       ter*]; for here comes the trout that must be caught with tickling.
                                                                  [*Exit.*]

Enter MALVOLIO

---

1. *sheep-biter*] A contemptuous term derived from a dog that worries sheep by biting.
2. *my metal of India*] my treasure of gold.

MAL.   'T is but fortune; all is fortune. Maria once told me she[3] did affect me: and I have heard herself come thus near, that, should she fancy, it should be one of my complexion. Besides, she uses me with a more exalted respect than any one else that follows her. What should I think on 't?

SIR TO.   Here's an overweening rogue!

FAB.   O, peace! Contemplation makes a rare turkey-cock of him: how he jets under his advanced plumes!

SIR AND.   'Slight, I could so beat the rogue!

SIR TO.   Peace, I say.

MAL.   To be Count Malvolio!

SIR TO.   Ah, rogue!

SIR AND.   Pistol him, pistol him.

SIR TO.   Peace, peace!

MAL.   There is example for 't; the lady of the Strachy married the yeoman of the wardrobe.

SIR AND.   Fie on him Jezebel!

FAB.   O, peace! now he 's deeply in: look how imagination blows him.

MAL.   Having been three months married to her, sitting in my state, —

SIR TO.   O, for a stone-bow,[4] to hit him in the eye!

MAL.   Calling my officers about me, in my branched velvet[5] gown; having come from a day-bed, where I have left Olivia sleeping, —

SIR TO.   Fire and brimstone!

FAB.   O, peace, peace!

MAL.   And then to have the humour of state; and after a demure travel of regard, telling them I know my place as I would they should do theirs, to ask for my kinsman Toby, —

SIR TO.   Bolts and shackles!

FAB.   O, peace, peace, peace! now, now.

MAL.   Seven of my people, with an obedient start, make out for him: I frown the while; and perchance wind up my watch, or play with my — some rich jewel. Toby approaches; courtesies there to me, —

SIR TO.   Shall this fellow live?

FAB.   Though our silence be drawn from us with cars,[6] yet peace.

MAL.   I extend my hand to him thus, quenching my familiar smile with an austere regard of control, —

---

3. *she*] i. e., Olivia, Maria's mistress.
4. *stone-bow*] a cross-bow from which stones were shot.
5. *branched velvet*] velvet ornamented with patterns of leaves and flowers.
6. *cars*] as in teams of horses.

SIR TO.   And does not Toby take you a blow o' the lips then?

MAL.   Saying, "Cousin Toby, my fortunes having cast me on your niece give me this prerogative of speech,"—

SIR TO.   What, what?

MAL.   "You must amend your drunkenness."

SIR TO.   Out, scab!

FAB.   Nay, patience, or we break the sinews of our plot.

MAL.   "Besides, you waste the treasure of your time with a foolish knight,"—

SIR AND.   That's me, I warrant you.

MAL.   "One Sir Andrew,"—

SIR AND.   I knew 't was I; for many do call me fool.

MAL.   What employment[7] have we here?   [*Taking up the letter.*]

FAB.   Now is the woodcock near the gin.[8]

SIR TO.   O, peace! and the spirit of humours intimate reading aloud to him!

MAL.   By my life, this is my lady's hand: these be her very C's, her U's, and her T's; and thus makes she her great P's. It is, in contempt of question, her hand.

SIR AND.   Her C's, her U's and her T's: why that?

MAL. [*Reads*]   To the unknown beloved, this, and my good wishes:—her very phrases! By your leave, wax. Soft! and the impressure her Lucrece,[9] with which she uses to seal: 't is my lady. To whom should this be?

FAB.   This wins him, liver and all.

MAL. [*Reads*]   Jove knows I love:
                            But who?
                         Lips, do not move;
                         No man must know.

"No man must know." What follows? the numbers altered! "No man must know:" if this should be thee, Malvolio?

SIR TO.   Marry, hang thee, brock![10]

---

7. *employment*] work, business.

8. *gin*] snare.

9. *impressure her Lucrece*] the impression on the letter's sealing wax was made by a seal bearing the figure of the Roman matron Lucrece.

10. *brock*] badger.

MAL. [*Reads*]   I may command where I adore;
                        But silence, like a Lucrece knife,
                        With bloodless stroke my heart doth gore:
                        M, O, A, I, doth sway my life.

FAB.   A fustian riddle!

SIR TO.   Excellent wench, say I.

MAL.   "M, O, A, I, doth sway my life." Nay, but first, let me see, let me
see, let me see.

FAB.   What dish o' poison has she dressed him!

SIR TO.   And with what wing the staniel checks[11] at it!

MAL.   "I may command where I adore." Why, she may command me:
I serve her; she is my lady. Why, this is evident to any formal
capacity;[12] there is no obstruction in this: and the end, — what
should that alphabetical position portend? If I could make that
resemble something in me, — Softly! M, O, A, I, —

SIR TO.   O, ay, make up that: he is now at a cold scent.

FAB.   Sowter will cry upon 't for all this, though it be as rank as a fox.[13]

MAL.   M, — Malvolio; M, — why, that begins my name.

FAB.   Did not I say he would work it out? the cur is excellent at faults.

MAL.   M, — but then there is no consonancy in the sequel; that suffers
under probation: A should follow, but O does.

FAB.   And O shall end, I hope.

SIR TO.   Ay, or I 'll cudgel him, and make him cry O!

MAL.   And then I comes behind.

FAB.   Ay, an you had any eye behind you, you might see more detrac-
tion at your heels than fortunes before you.

MAL.   M, O, A, I; this simulation is not as the former: and yet, to crush
this a little, it would bow to me, for every one of these letters are
in my name. Soft! here follows prose.

[*Reads*]   If this fall into thy hand, revolve. In my stars I am above thee;
but be not afraid of greatness: some are born great, some achieve greatness, and some have greatness thrust upon 'em. Thy Fates open their
hands; let thy blood and spirit embrace them; and, to inure thyself to
what thou art like to be, cast thy humble slough and appear fresh. Be

---

11. *staniel checks*] staniel is a kind of hawk, and the verb "check" is a technical term in
falconry, applied to the hawk's sudden swoop in flight when she catches sight of
winged prey.

12. *formal capacity*] well-regulated mind.

13. *Sowter . . . fox*] "Sowter" (i. e., botcher, cobbler) is used as the name of a bad, dull
hound. So poor a cur, although capable of any amount of bungling, must take this scent.

opposite with a kinsman, surly with servants; let thy tongue tang[14] arguments of state; put thyself into the trick of singularity: she thus advises thee that sighs for thee. Remember who commended thy yellow stockings, and wished to see thee ever cross-gartered:[15] I say, remember. Go to, thou art made, if thou desirest to be so; if not, let me see thee a steward still, the fellow of servants, and not worthy to touch Fortune's fingers. Farewell. She that would alter services with thee,

THE FORTUNATE-UNHAPPY.

Daylight and champain[16] discovers not more: this is open. I will be proud, I will read politic authors, I will baffle Sir Toby, I will wash off gross acquaintance, I will be point-devise[17] the very man. I do not now fool myself, to let imagination jade me; for every reason excites to this, that my lady loves me. She did commend my yellow stockings of late, she did praise my leg being cross-gartered; and in this she manifests herself to my love, and with a kind of injunction drives me to these habits of her liking. I thank my stars I am happy. I will be strange, stout, in yellow stockings, and cross-gartered, even with the swiftness of putting on. Jove and my stars be praised! Here is yet a postscript.

[Reads]   Thou canst not choose but know who I am. If thou entertainest my love, let it appear in thy smiling; thy smiles become thee well; therefore in my presence still smile, dear my sweet, I prithee.

Jove, I thank thee: I will smile; I will do every thing that thou wilt have me.   [Exit.]

FAB.   I will not give my part of this sport for a pension of thousands to be paid from the Sophy.[18]

SIR TO.   I could marry this wench for this device,—

SIR AND.   So could I too.

SIR TO.   And ask no other dowry with her but such another jest.

SIR AND.   Nor I neither.

FAB.   Here comes my noble gull-catcher.[19]

Re-enter MARIA

---

14. tang] ring or sound loud with.
15. yellow stockings and . . . cross-gartered] Yellow was at the time a popular colour of stockings; men of fashion were in the habit of wearing their garters crossed both above and below the knee, with the ends fastened together behind the knee.
16. champain] open country.
17. point-devise] exactly (point-by-point) as the letter describes.
18. the Sophy] the Shah of Persia.
19. gull-catcher] fool-catcher.

SIR TO. Wilt thou set thy foot o' my neck?

SIR AND. Or o' mine either?

SIR TO. Shall I play my freedom at tray-trip,[20] and become thy bond-slave?

SIR AND. I' faith, or I either?

SIR TO. Why, thou has put him in such a dream, that when the image of it leaves him he must run mad.

MAR. Nay, but say true; does it work upon him?

SIR TO. Like aqua-vitæ[21] with a midwife.

MAR. If you will then see the fruits of the sport, mark his first approach before my lady: he will come to her in yellow stockings, and 't is a colour she abhors, and cross-gartered, a fashion she detests; and he will smile upon her, which will now be so unsuitable to her disposition, being addicted to a melancholy as she is, that it cannot but turn him into a notable contempt. If you will see it, follow me.

SIR TO. To the gates of Tartar,[22] thou most excellent devil of wit!

SIR AND. I 'll make one too. [*Exeunt.*]

ACT III

SCENE I. OLIVIA'S *garden.*

Enter VIOLA, *and* Clown *with a tabor*

VIO. Save thee, friend, and thy music: dost thou live by thy tabor?

CLO. No, sir, I live by the church.

VIO. Art thou a churchman?

CLO. No such matter, sir: I do live by the church; for I do live at my house, and my house doth stand by the church.

VIO. So thou mayst say, the king lies by a beggar, if a beggar dwell near him; or, the church stands by the tabor, if thy tabor stand by the church.

---

20. *tray-trip*] a game of dice in which rolling a three ("tray") was desirable.
21. *aqua-vitæ*] strong spirits.
22. *Tartar*] Hell.

CLO.   You have said, sir. To see this age! A sentence[1] is but a cheveril[2]
       glove to a good wit: how quickly the wrong side may be turned
       outward!
VIO.   Nay, that 's certain; they that dally nicely with words may quick-
       ly make them wanton.
CLO.   I would, therefore, my sister had had no name, sir.
VIO.   Why, man?
CLO.   Why, sir, her name 's a word; and to dally with that word might
       make my sister wanton. But indeed words are very rascals since
       bonds disgraced them.
VIO.   Thy reason, man?
CLO.   Troth, sir, I can yield you none without words; and words are
       grown so false, I am loath to prove reason with them.
VIO.   I warrant thou art a merry fellow and carest for nothing.
CLO.   Not so, sir, I do care for something; but in my conscience, sir, I
       do not care for you: if that be to care for nothing, sir, I would it
       would make you invisible.
VIO.   Art not thou the Lady Olivia's fool?
CLO.   No, indeed, sir; the Lady Olivia has no folly: she will keep no
       fool, sir, till she be married; and fools are as like husbands as
       pilchards[3] are to herrings; the husband 's the bigger: I am indeed
       not her fool, but her corrupter of words.
VIO.   I saw thee late at the Count Orsino's.
CLO.   Foolery, sir, does walk about the orb like the sun, it shines every
       where. I would be sorry, sir, but the fool should be as oft with your
       master as with my mistress: I think I saw your wisdom there.
VIO.   Nay, an thou pass upon me,[4] I 'll no more with thee. Hold,
       there 's expenses for thee.
CLO.   Now Jove, in his next commodity of hair, send thee a beard!
VIO.   By my troth, I 'll tell thee, I am almost sick for one; [Aside]
       though I would not have it grow on my chin. Is thy lady within?
CLO.   Would not a pair of these have bred, sir?[5]
VIO.   Yes, being kept together and put to use.
CLO.   I would play Lord Pandarus of Phrygia, sir, to bring a Cressida
       to this Troilus.

---

1. *sentence*] maxim.
2. *cheveril*] very flexible leather from roebuck.
3. *pilchards*] or pilchers; fish resembling herrings.
4. *an . . . me*] if you make jokes at my expense.
5. *Would . . . bred*] Viola has given the clown two coins, and he wonders that they did not
   multiply (i.e., that his tip was not bigger).

VIO.   I understand you, sir; 't is well begged.

CLO.   The matter, I hope, is not great, sir, begging but a beggar: Cressida was a beggar. My lady is within, sir. I will construe to them whence you come; who you are and what you would are out of my welkin,[6] I might say "element," but the word is over-worn.

[*Exit.*]

VIO.   This fellow is wise enough to play the fool;
And to do that well craves a kind of wit:
He must observe their mood on whom he jests,
The quality of persons, and the time,
And, like the haggard, check at every feather[7]
That comes before his eye. This is a practice
As full of labour as a wise man's art:
For folly that he wisely shows is fit;
But wise men, folly-fall'n, quite taint their wit.

Enter SIR TOBY, *and* SIR ANDREW

SIR TO.   Save you, gentleman.

VIO.   And you, sir.

SIR AND.   Dieu vous garde, monsieur.

VIO.   Et vous aussi; votre serviteur.[8]

SIR AND.   I hope, sir, you are; and I am yours.

SIR TO.   Will you encounter[9] the house? my niece is desirous you should enter, if your trade be to her.

VIO.   I am bound to your niece, sir; I mean, she is the list[10] of my voyage.

SIR TO.   Taste[11] your legs, sir; put them to motion.

VIO.   My legs do better understand me, sir, than I understand what you mean by bidding me taste my legs.

SIR TO.   I mean, to go, sir, to enter.

VIO.   I will answer you with gait and entrance. But we are prevented.

Enter OLIVIA *and* MARIA

Most excellent accomplished lady, the heavens rain odours on you!

---

6. *welkin*] sky.
7. *like . . . feather*] see note 11 on page 32; a haggard is a wild, untrained hawk.
8. *Dieu . . . serviteur*] (Sir Andrew): God keep you, sir.
   (Viola): And you, too; [I am] your servant.
9. *encounter*] enter.
10. *list*] bound, limit.
11. *Taste*] Try.

SIR AND.   That youth 's a rare courtier: "Rain odours"; well.

VIO.   My matter hath no voice, lady, but to your own most pregnant
and vouchsafed ear.

SIR AND.   "Odours," "pregnant," and "vouchsafed": I 'll get 'em all
three all ready.

OLI.   Let the garden door be shut, and leave me to my hearing.
[*Exeunt* SIR TOBY, SIR ANDREW, *and* MARIA.] Give me your hand,
sir.

VIO.   My duty, madam, and most humble service.

OLI.   What is your name?

VIO.   Cesario is your servant's name, fair princess.

OLI.   My servant, sir! 'T was never merry world
Since lowly feigning was call'd compliment:
You 're servant to the Count Orsino, youth.

VIO.   And he is yours, and his must needs be yours:
Your servant's servant is your servant, madam.

OLI.   For him, I think not on him: for his thoughts,
Would they were blanks, rather than fill'd with me!

VIO.   Madam, I come to whet your gentle thoughts
On his behalf.

OLI.   O, by your leave, I pray you;
I bade you never speak again of him:
But, would you undertake another suit,
I had rather hear you to solicit that
Than music from the spheres.

VIO.   Dear lady,—

OLI.   Give me leave, beseech you. I did send,
After the last enchantment you did here,
A ring in chase of you: so did I abuse
Myself, my servant and, I fear me, you:
Under your hard construction must I sit,
To force that on you, in a shameful cunning,
Which you knew none of yours: what might you think?
Have you not set mine honour at the stake
And baited it with all the unmuzzled thoughts
That tyrannous heart can think? To one of your receiving
Enough is shown: a cypress,[12] not a bosom,
Hides my heart. So, let me hear you speak.

---

12. *cypress*] mourning garments.

VIO.   I pity you.

OLI.   That's a degree to love.

VIO.   No, not a grize;[13] for 't is a vulgar proof,
       That very oft we pity enemies.

OLI.   Why, then, methinks, 't is time to smile again.
       O world, how apt the poor are to be proud!
       If one should be a prey, how much the better
       To fall before the lion than the wolf!   [*Clock strikes.*]
       The clock upbraids me with the waste of time.
       Be not afraid, good youth, I will not have you:
       And yet, when wit and youth is come to harvest,
       Your wife is like to reap a proper man:
       There lies your way, due west.

VIO.   Then westward-ho!
       Grace and good disposition attend your ladyship!
       You 'll nothing, madam, to my lord by me?

OLI.   Stay:
       I prithee, tell me what thou think'st of me.

VIO.   That you do think you are not what you are.

OLI.   If I think so, I think the same of you.

VIO.   Then think you right: I am not what I am.

OLI.   I would you were as I would have you be!

VIO.   Would it be better, madam, than I am?
       I wish it might, for now I am your fool.

OLI.   O, what a deal of scorn looks beautiful
       In the contempt and anger of his lip!
       A murderous guilt shows not itself more soon
       Than love that would seem hid: love's night is noon.
       Cesario, by the roses of the spring,
       By maidenhood, honour, truth and every thing,
       I love thee so, that, maugre[14] all thy pride,
       Nor wit nor reason can my passion hide.
       Do not extort thy reasons from this clause,
       For that I woo, thou therefore hast no cause;
       But rather reason thus with reason fetter,
       Love sought is good, but given unsought is better.

VIO.   By innocence I swear, and by my youth,
       I have one heart, one bosom and one truth,

---

13. *grize*] step.
14. *maugre*] in spite of.

And that no woman has; nor. never none
Shall mistress be of it, save I alone.
And so adieu, good madam: never more
Will I my master's tears to you deplore.

OLI.   Yet come again; for thou perhaps mayst move
That heart, which now abhors, to like his love.   [*Exeunt.*]

SCENE II. OLIVIA'S *house*.

Enter SIR TOBY, SIR ANDREW, *and* FABIAN

SIR AND.   No, faith, I 'll not stay a jot longer.

SIR TO.   Thy reason, dear venom, give thy reason.

FAB.   You must needs yield your reason, Sir Andrew.

SIR AND.   Marry, I saw your niece do more favours to the count's serv-
   ing-man than ever she bestowed upon me; I saw 't i' the orchard.

SIR TO.   Did she see thee the while, old boy? tell me that.

SIR AND.   As plain as I see you now.

FAB.   This was a great argument of love in her toward you.

SIR AND.   'Slight, will you make an ass o' me?

FAB.   I will prove it legitimate, sir, upon the oaths of judgement and
   reason.

SIR TO.   And they have been grand-jurymen since before Noah was a
   sailor.

FAB.   She did show favour to the youth in your sight only to exasperate
   you, to awake your dormouse valour, to put fire in your heart, and
   brimstone in your liver. You should then have accosted her; and
   with some excellent jests, fire-new from the mint, you should have
   banged the youth into dumbness. This was looked for at your hand,
   and this was balked: the double gilt of this opportunity you let time
   wash off, and you are now sailed into the north of my lady's opinion; where you will hang like an icicle on a Dutchman's beard,[1]

----

1. *like an icicle . . . beard*] This simile seems to have been suggested by an English trans-
   lation of a Dutch account of the discovery by a Dutchman, Willem Barents, in 1596,
   of Nova Zembla, and of the explorer's sufferings from extremity of cold. The transla-
   tion seems to have been first published in 1598, though no copy earlier than 1609 has
   been met with.

unless you do redeem it by some laudable attempt either of valour or policy.

SIR AND.   An 't be any way, it must be with valour; for policy I hate: I had as lief be a Brownist[2] as a politician.

SIR TO.   Why, then, build me thy fortunes upon the basis of valour. Challenge me the count's youth to fight with him; hurt him in eleven places: my niece shall take note of it; and assure thyself, there is no love-broker in the world can more prevail in man's commendation with woman than report of valour.

FAB.   There is no way but this, Sir Andrew.

SIR AND.   Will either of you bear me a challenge to him?

SIR TO.   Go, write it in a martial hand; be curst[3] and brief; it is no matter how witty, so it be eloquent and full of invention: taunt him with the license of ink: if thou thou'st[4] him some thrice, it shall not be amiss; and as many lies as will lie in thy sheet of paper, although the sheet were big enough for the bed of Ware[5] in England, set 'em down: go, about it. Let there be gall enough in thy ink, though thou write with a goose-pen, no matter: about it.

SIR AND.   Where shall I find you?

SIR TO.   We 'll call thee at the cubiculo:[6] go.   [*Exit* SIR ANDREW.]

FAB.   This is a dear manakin to you, Sir Toby.

SIR TO.   I have been dear to him, lad, some two thousand strong, or so.

FAB.   We shall have a rare letter from him: but you 'll not deliver 't?

SIR TO.   Never trust me, then; and by all means stir on the youth to an answer. I think oxen and wainropes[7] cannot hale[8] them together. For Andrew, if he were opened, and you find so much blood in his liver as will clog the foot of a flea, I 'll eat the rest of the anatomy.

FAB.   And his opposite, the youth, bears in his visage no great presage of cruelty.

Enter MARIA

---

2. *Brownist*] a member of the religious sect of Puritan separatists or independents, which was founded by Robert Brown about 1580, and rapidly spread in secret, despite efforts made to suppress it.

3. *curst*] waspish, bellicose.

4. *thou thou'st*] To address a person as "thou" was held to be insulting.

5. *bed of Ware*] A giant bed, capable of holding twelve persons, long gave notoriety to an inn at Ware, a village in Hertfordshire.

6. *the cubiculo*] Sir Toby's bombastic periphrasis for Sir Andrew's lodging or bedroom.

7. *wainropes*] cart ropes.

8. *hale*] pull, drag.

SIR TO.   Look, where the youngest wren of nine comes.[9]

MAR.   If you desire the spleen, and will laugh yourselves into stitches, follow me. Yond gull[10] Malvolio is turned heathen, a very renegado; for there is no Christian, that means to be saved by believing rightly, can ever believe such impossible passages of grossness.[11] He 's in yellow stockings.

SIR TO.   And cross-gartered?

MAR.   Most villanously; like a pedant that keeps a school i' the church. I have dogged him, like his murderer. He does obey every point of the letter that I dropped to betray him: he does smile his face into more lines than is in the new map with the augmentation of the Indies:[12] you have not seen such a thing as 't is. I can hardly forbear hurling things at him. I know my lady will strike him: if she do, he 'll smile and take 't for a great favour.

SIR TO.   Come, bring us, bring us where he is.   [*Exeunt.*]

SCENE III. *A street.*

Enter SEBASTIAN *and* ANTONIO

SEB.   I would not by my will have troubled you;
        But, since you make your pleasure of your pains,
        I will no further chide you.

ANT.   I could not stay behind you: my desire,
        More sharp than filed steel, did spur me forth;
        And not all love to see you, though so much
        As might have drawn one to a longer voyage,
        But jealousy what might befall your travel,
        Being skilless in these parts; which to a stranger,
        Unguided and unfriended, often prove

---

9. *wren of nine*] The allusion is to Maria's diminutive stature. The wren lays at a time nine or ten eggs, usually of descending size.

10. *gull*] fool; someone easily tricked.

11. *passages of grossness*] acts of absurdity.

12. *new map . . . Indies*] A new map of the world was made in 1599 by Emmerie Mollineux. It is multilineal, and plainly marks recent exploration in both the East and the West hemispheres.

Rough and unhospitable: my willing love,
The rather by these arguments of fear,
Set forth in your pursuit.

SEB.   My kind Antonio,
I can no other answer make but thanks,
And thanks; and ever. . . . oft good turns
Are shuffled off with such uncurrent pay:
But, were my worth as is my conscience firm,
You should find better dealing. What 's to do?
Shall we go see the reliques of this town?

ANT.   To-morrow, sir: best first go see your lodging.

SEB.   I am not weary, and 't is long to night:
I pray you, let us satisfy our eyes
With the memorials and the things of fame
That do renown this city.

ANT.   Would you 'ld pardon me;
I do not without danger walk these streets:
Once, in a sea-fight, 'gainst the count his galleys
I did some service; of such note indeed,
That were I ta'en here it would scarce be answer'd.

SEB.   Belike you slew great number of his people.

ANT.   The offence is not of such a bloody nature;
Albeit the quality of the time and quarrel
Might well have given us bloody argument.
It might have since been answer'd in repaying
What we took from them; which, for traffic's sake,
Most of our city did: only myself stood out;
For which, if I be lapsed[1] in this place,
I shall pay dear.

SEB.   Do not then walk too open.

ANT.   It doth not fit me. Hold, sir, here 's my purse.
In the south suburbs, at the Elephant,[2]
Is best to lodge: I will bespeak our diet,
Whiles you beguile the time and feed your knowledge
With viewing of the town: there shall you have me.

SEB.   Why I your purse?

ANT.   Haply your eye shall light upon some toy
You have desire to purchase; and your store,

---

1. *lapsed*] caught, surprised.
2. *Elephant*] an inn.

I think, is not for idle markets, sir.

SEB. I 'll be your purse-bearer and leave you
      For an hour.

ANT.   To the Elephant.

SEB.   I do remember.   [*Exeunt.*]

SCENE IV. OLIVIA'S *garden.*

Enter OLIVIA *and* MARIA

OLI. I have sent after him: he[1] says he 'll come;
      How shall I feast him? what bestow of him?
      For youth is bought more oft than begg'd or borrow'd.
      I speak too loud.
      Where is Malvolio? he is sad and civil,
      And suits well for a servant with my fortunes:
      Where is Malvolio?

MAR. He 's coming, madam; but in very strange manner. He is, sure,
      possessed, madam.

OLI. Why, what 's the matter? does he rave?

MAR. No, madam, he does nothing but smile: your ladyship were
      best to have some guard about you, if he come; for, sure, the man
      is tainted in 's wits.

OLI. Go call him hither. [*Exit* MARIA.] I am as mad as he,
      If sad and merry madness equal be.

Re-enter MARIA, *with* MALVOLIO

      How now, Malvolio!

MAL. Sweet lady, ho, ho.

OLI. Smilest thou?
      I sent for thee upon a sad occasion.

MAL. Sad, lady? I could be sad: this does make some obstruction in
      the blood, this cross-gartering; but what of that? if it please the eye
      of one, it is with me as the very true sonnet is, "Please one, and
      please all."

---

1. *he*] Cesario (i.e., Viola).

OLI. Why, how dost thou, man? what is the matter with thee?

MAL. Not black in my mind, though yellow in my legs. It did come to his hands, and commands shall be executed: I think we do know the sweet Roman hand.

OLI. Wilt thou go to bed, Malvolio?

MAL. To bed! ay, sweet-heart, and I 'll come to thee.

OLI. God comfort thee! Why dost thou smile so and kiss thy hand so oft?

MAR. How do you, Malvolio?

MAL. At your request! yes; nightingales answer daws.

MAR. Why appear you with this ridiculous boldness before my lady?

MAL. "Be not afraid of greatness": 't was well writ.

OLI. What meanest thou by that, Malvolio?

MAL. "Some are born great,"—

OLI. Ha!

MAL. "Some achieve greatness,"—

OLI. What sayest thou?

MAL. "And some have greatness thrust upon them."

OLI. Heaven restore thee!

MAL. "Remember who commended thy yellow stockings,"—

OLI. Thy yellow stockings!

MAL. "And wished to see thee cross-gartered."

OLI. Cross-gartered!

MAL. "Go to, thou art made, if thou desirest to be so";—

OLI. Am I made?

MAL. "If not, let me see thee a servant still."

OLI. Why, this is very midsummer madness.

Enter Servant

SER. Madam, the young gentleman of the Count Orsino's is returned: I could hardly entreat him back: he attends your lady-ship's pleasure.

OLI. I 'll come to him. [*Exit* Servant.] Good Maria, let this fellow be looked to. Where 's my cousin Toby? Let some of my people have a special care of him: I would not have him miscarry for the half of my dowry. [*Exeunt* OLIVIA *and* MARIA.]

MAL. O, ho! do you come near[2] me now? no worse man than Sir Toby to look to me! This concurs directly with the letter: she sends

---

2. *come near*] understand.

him on purpose, that I may appear stubborn to him; for she incites me to that in the letter. "Cast thy humble slough," says she; "be opposite with a kinsman, surly with servants; let thy tongue tang with arguments of state; put thyself into the trick of singularity"; and consequently sets down the manner how; as, a sad face, a reverend carriage, a slow tongue, in the habit of some sir of note, and so forth. I have limed[3] her; but it is Jove's doing, and Jove make me thankful! And when she went away now, "Let this fellow be looked to": fellow! not Malvolio, nor after my degree, but fellow. Why, every thing adheres together, that no dram of a scruple, no scruple of a scruple, no obstacle, no incredulous or unsafe circumstance— What can be said? Nothing that can be can come between me and the full prospect of my hopes. Well, Jove, not I, is the doer of this, and he is to be thanked.

Re-enter MARIA, *with* SIR TOBY *and* FABIAN

SIR TO.   Which way is he, in the name of sanctity? If all the devils of hell be drawn in little, and Legion[4] himself possessed him, yet I 'll speak to him.

FAB.   Here he is, here he is. How is 't with you, sir? how is 't with you, man?

MAL.   Go off; I discard you: let me enjoy my private: go off.

MAR.   Lo, how hollow the fiend speaks within him! did not I tell you? Sir Toby, my lady prays you to have a care of him.

MAL.   Ah, ha! does she so?

SIR TO.   Go to, go to; peace, peace; we must deal gently with him: let me alone. How do you, Malvolio? how is 't with you? What, man! defy the devil: consider, he 's an enemy to mankind.

MAL.   Do you know what you say?

MAR.   La you, an you speak ill of the devil, how he takes it at heart! Pray God, he be not bewitched!

FAB.   Carry his water to the wise woman.

MAR.   Marry, and it shall be done to-morrow morning, if I live. My lady would not lose him for more than I 'll say.

MAL.   How now, mistress!

MAR.   O Lord!

---

3. *limed*] caught, ensnared.
4. *Legion*] in the New Testament Christ exorcises a demon who calls himself "Legion: for we are many" (Mark 5:9).

SIR TO.   Prithee, hold thy peace; this is not the way: do you not see
      you move him? let me alone with him.
FAB.   No way but gentleness; gently, gently: the fiend is rough, and
      will not be roughly used.
SIR TO.   Why, how now, my bawcock! how dost thou, chuck?
MAL.   Sir!
SIR TO.   Ay, Biddy,[5] come with me. What, man! 't is not for gravity to
      play at cherry-pit with Satan: hang him, foul collier![6]
MAR.   Get him to say his prayers, good Sir Toby, get him to pray.
MAL.   My prayers, minx!
MAR.   No, I warrant you, he will not hear of godliness.
MAL.   Go, hang yourselves all! you are idle shallow things: I am not of
      your element: you shall know more hereafter.   [*Exit.*]
SIR TO.   Is 't possible?
FAB.   If this were played upon a stage now, I could condemn it as an
      improbable fiction.
SIR TO.   His very genius hath taken the infection of the device, man.
MAR.   Nay, pursue him now, lest the device take air and taint.
FAB.   Why, we shall make him mad indeed.
MAR.   The house will be the quieter.
SIR TO.   Come, we 'll have him in a dark room and bound. My niece
      is already in the belief that he 's mad: we may carry it thus, for our
      pleasure and his penance, till our very pastime, tired out of breath,
      prompt us to have mercy on him: at which time we will bring the
      device to the bar and crown thee for a finder of madmen.[7] But see,
      but see.

Enter SIR ANDREW

FAB.   More matter for a May morning.[8]
SIR AND.   Here 's the challenge, read it: I warrant there 's vinegar and
      pepper in 't.
FAB.   Is 't so saucy?
SIR AND.   Ay, is 't, I warrant him: do but read.

---

5. *Biddy*] term used to call chickens.
6. *play . . . collier!*] cherry-pit was a children's game played by throwing cherry pits into a
   little hole; the references to Satan and the collier allude to the proverb "Like will to
   like, as the devil with the collier," a digger or seller of coals.
7. *finder of madmen*] those appointed to report on persons suspected of madness.
8. *More . . . morning*] On May Day it was the custom to perform comic interludes or fan-
   tastic dances.

SIR TO.   Give me. [*Reads*] Youth, whatsoever thou art, thou art but a scurvy fellow.

FAB.   Good, and valiant.

SIR TO.   [*Reads*] Wonder not, nor admire not in thy mind, why I do call thee so, for I will show thee no reason for 't.

FAB.   A good note; that keeps you from the blow of the law.

SIR TO.   [*Reads*] Thou comest to the lady Olivia, and in my sight she uses thee kindly: but thou liest in thy throat; that is not the matter I challenge thee for.

FAB.   Very brief, and to exceeding good sense—less.

SIR TO.   [*Reads*] I will waylay thee going home; where if it be thy chance to kill me,—

FAB.   Good.

SIR TO.   [*Reads*] Thou killest me like a rogue and a villain.

FAB.   Still you keep o' the windy side of the law: good.

SIR TO.   [*Reads*] Fare thee well; and God have mercy upon one of our souls! He may have mercy upon mine; but my hope is better, and so look to thyself. Thy friend, as thou usest him, and thy sworn enemy,

ANDREW AGUECHEEK.

If this letter move him not, his legs cannot: I 'll give 't him.

MAR.   You may have very fit occasion for 't: he is now in some commerce with my lady, and will by and by depart.

SIR TO.   Go, Sir Andrew; scout me for him at the corner of the orchard like a bum-baily:[9] so soon as ever thou seest him, draw; and, as thou drawest, swear horrible; for it comes to pass oft that a terrible oath, with a swaggering accent sharply twanged off, gives manhood more approbation than ever proof itself would have earned him. Away!

SIR AND.   Nay, let me alone for swearing.   [*Exit.*]

SIR TO.   Now will not I deliver his letter: for the behaviour of the young gentleman gives him out to be of good capacity and breeding; his employment between his lord and my niece confirms no less: therefore this letter, being so excellently ignorant, will breed no terror in the youth: he will find it comes from a clodpole. But, sir, I will deliver his challenge by word of mouth; set upon Aguecheek a notable report of valour; and drive the gentleman, as I know his youth will aptly receive it, into a most hideous opinion

---

9. *bum-baily*] junior officer employed in making arrests.

of his rage, skill, fury, and impetuosity. This will so fright them
both, that they will kill one another by the look, like cockatrices.[10]

Re-enter OLIVIA, *with* VIOLA

FAB.   Here he comes with your niece: give them way till he take leave,
and presently after him.

SIR TO.   I will meditate the while upon some horrid message for a
challenge.   [*Exeunt* SIR TOBY, FABIAN, *and* MARIA.]

OLI.   I have said too much unto a heart of stone,
And laid mine honour too unchary out:
There 's something in me that reproves my fault;
But such a headstrong potent fault it is,
That it but mocks reproof.

VIO.   With the same 'haviour that your passion bears
Goes on my master's grief.

OLI.   Here, wear this jewel for me, 't is my picture;
Refuse it not; it hath no tongue to vex you;
And I beseech you come again to-morrow.
What shall you ask of me that I 'll deny,
That honour saved may upon asking give?

VIO.   Nothing but this;—your true love for my master.

OLI.   How with mine honour may I give him that
Which I have given to you?

VIO.   I will acquit you.

OLI.   Well, come again to-morrow: fare thee well:
A fiend like thee might bear my soul to hell.   [*Exit.*]

Re-enter SIR TOBY *and* FABIAN

SIR TO.   Gentleman, God save thee.

VIO.   And you, sir.

SIR TO.   That defence thou hast, betake thee to 't: of what nature the
wrongs are thou hast done him, I know not; but thy intercepter,
full of despite, bloody as the hunter, attends thee at the orchard-
end: dismount thy tuck,[11] be yare[12] in thy preparation, for thy
assailant is quick, skilful and deadly.

VIO.   You mistake, sir; I am sure no man hath any quarrel to me: my

---

10. *cockatrices*] imaginary birds, supposed to be hatched from cocks' eggs, and that could
kill with a look.

11. *dismount thy tuck*] draw thy sword or rapier.

12. *yare*] ready, brisk.

remembrance is very free and clear from any image of offence
done to any man.

SIR TO.   You 'll find it otherwise, I assure you: therefore, if you hold
your life at any price, betake you to your guard; for your opposite
hath in him what youth, strength, skill and wrath can furnish man
withal.

VIO.   I pray you, sir, what is he?

SIR TO.   He is knight, dubbed with unhatched rapier and on carpet
consideration;[13] but he is a devil in private brawl: souls and bodies
hath he divorced three; and his incensement at this moment is so
implacable, that satisfaction can be none but by pangs of death
and sepulchre. Hob, nob,[14] is his word; give 't or take 't.

VIO.   I will return again into the house and desire some conduct of
the lady. I am no fighter. I have heard of some kind of men that
put quarrels purposely on others, to taste their valour: belike this
is a man of that quirk.

SIR TO.   Sir, no; his indignation derives itself out of a very competent
injury: therefore, get you on and give him his desire. Back you
shall not to the house, unless you undertake that with me which
with as much safety you might answer him: therefore, on, or strip
your sword stark naked; for meddle you must, that 's certain, or
forswear to wear iron about you.

VIO.   This is as uncivil as strange. I beseech you, do me this courteous
office, as to know of the knight what my offence to him is: it is
something of my negligence, nothing of my purpose.

SIR TO.   I will do so. Signior Fabian, stay you by this gentleman till
my return.   [Exit.]

VIO.   Pray you, sir, do you know of this matter?

FAB.   I know the knight is incensed against you, even to a mortal arbitrement;[15] but nothing of the circumstance more.

VIO.   I beseech you, what manner of man is he?

FAB.   Nothing of that wonderful promise, to read him by his form, as
you are like to find him in the proof of his valour. He is, indeed,
sir, the most skilful, bloody and fatal opposite that you could pos-

---

13. *knight . . . on carpet consideration*] a carpet knight was one whose title was not derived
from military service; an "unhatched rapier" is a rapier that has not been used in military combat.

14. *Hob, nob*] "Hob" is a corruption of "have," and the expression here means "have or
have not," "hit or miss."

15. *arbitrement*] decision.

sibly have found in any part of Illyria. Will you walk towards him? I will make your peace with him if I can.

VIO. I shall be much bound to you for 't: I am one that had rather go with sir priest than sir knight: I care not who knows so much of my mettle. [*Exeunt.*]

Re-enter SIR TOBY, *with* SIR ANDREW

SIR TO. Why, man, he 's a very devil; I have not seen such a firago.[16] I had a pass with him, rapier, scabbard and all, and he gives me the stuck in[17] with such a mortal motion, that it is inevitable; and on the answer, he pays you as surely as your feet hit the ground they step on. They say he has been fencer to the Sophy.

SIR AND. Pox on 't, I 'll not meddle with him.

SIR TO. Ay, but he will not now be pacified: Fabian can scarce hold him yonder.

SIR AND. Plague on 't, an I thought he had been valiant and so cunning in fence, I 'ld have seen him damned ere I 'ld have challenged him. Let him let the matter slip, and I 'll give him my horse, grey Capilet.[18]

SIR TO. I 'll make the motion: stand here, make a good show on 't: this shall end without the perdition of souls. [*Aside*] Marry, I 'll ride your horse as well as I ride you.

Re-enter FABIAN *and* VIOLA

[*To* FAB.] I have his horse to take up the quarrel: I have persuaded him the youth 's a devil.

FAB. He is as horribly conceited of him; and pants and looks pale, as if a bear were at his heels.

SIR TO. [*To* VIO.] There's no remedy, sir; he will fight with you for 's oath sake: marry, he hath better bethought him of his quarrel, and he finds that now scarce to be worth talking of: therefore draw, for the supportance of his vow; he protests he will not hurt you.

VIO. [*Aside*] Pray God defend me! A little thing would make me tell them how much I lack of a man.

FAB. Give ground, if you see him furious.

SIR TO. Come, Sir Andrew, there 's no remedy; the gentleman will, for his honour's sake, have one bout with you; he cannot by the

---

16. *firago*] virago.

17. *stuck in*] Sir Toby's corruption of the Italian fencing term for thrust, "stoccata."

18. *Capilet*] apparently a diminutive, formed from "capul" or "caple," a north-country word for a horse.

    duello[19] avoid it: but he has promised me, as he is a gentleman and
    a soldier, he will not hurt you. Come on; to 't.

SIR AND.   Pray God, he keep his oath!

VIO.   I do assure you, 't is against my will.   *[They draw.]*

Enter Antonio

ANT.   Put up your sword. If this young gentleman
        Have done offence, I take the fault on me:
        If you offend him, I for him defy you.

SIR TO.   You, sir! why, what are you?

ANT.   One, sir, that for his love dares yet do more
        Than you have heard him brag to you he will.

SIR TO.   Nay, if you be an undertaker,[20] I am for you.   *[They draw.]*

Enter Officers

FAB.   O good Sir Toby, hold! here comes the officers.

SIR TO.   I 'll be with you anon.

VIO.   Pray, sir, put your sword up, if you please.

SIR AND.   Marry, will I, sir; and, for that I promised you, I 'll be as
    good as my word: he will bear you easily and reins well.[21]

FIRST OFF.   This is the man; do thy office.

SEC. OFF.   Antonio, I arrest thee at the suit of Count Orsino.

ANT.   You do mistake me, sir.

FIRST OFF.   No, sir, no jot; I know your favour well,
        Though now you have no sea-cap on your head.
        Take him away: he knows I know him well.

ANT.   I must obey. *[To* VIO.*]* This comes with seeking you:
        But there 's no remedy; I shall answer it.
        What will you do, now my necessity
        Makes me to ask you for my purse? It grieves me
        Much more for what I cannot do for you
        Than what befalls myself. You stand amazed;
        But be of comfort.

SEC. OFF.   Come, sir, away.

ANT.   I must entreat of you some of that money.

VIO.   What money, sir?
        For the fair kindness you have show'd me here,

---

19. *duello*] the code of the duel.
20. *undertaker*] an intermedler.
21. *he . . . well*] Sir Andrew refers to his horse.

And, part, being prompted by your present trouble,
Out of my lean and low ability
I 'll lend you something: my having[22] is not much;
I 'll make division of my present[23] with you:
Hold, there 's half my coffer.

ANT.   Will you deny me now?
Is 't possible that my deserts to you
Can lack persuasion? Do not tempt my misery,
Lest that it make me so unsound a man
As to upbraid you with those kindnesses
That I have done for you.

VIO.   I know of none;
Nor know I you by voice or any feature:
I hate ingratitude more in a man
Than lying vainness,[24] babbling drunkenness,
Or any taint of vice whose strong corruption
Inhabits our frail blood.

ANT.   O heavens themselves!

SEC. OFF.   Come, sir, I pray you, go.

ANT.   Let me speak a little. This youth that you see here
I snatch'd one half out of the jaws of death;
Relieved him with such sanctity of love;
And to his image, which methought did promise
Most venerable worth, did I devotion.

FIRST OFF.   What 's that to us? The time goes by: away!

ANT.   But O how vile an idol proves his god!
Thou hast, Sebastian, done good feature shame.
In nature there 's no blemish but the mind;
None can be call'd deform'd but the unkind:
Virtue is beauty; but the beauteous evil
Are empty trunks, o'erflourish'd by the devil.

FIRST OFF.   The man grows mad: away with him! Come, come, sir.

ANT.   Lead me on.   [*Exit with* Officers.]

VIO.   Methinks his words do from such passion fly,
That he believes himself: so do not I.
Prove true, imagination, O prove true,
That I, dear brother, be now ta'en for you!

---

22. *having*] property, fortune.
23. *my present*] my present store.
24. *lying vainness*] lying boastfulness.

SIR TO. Come hither, knight; come hither, Fabian: we 'll whisper
    o'er a couplet or two of most sage saws.
VIO. He named Sebastian: I my brother know
    Yet living in my glass; even such and so
    In favour was my brother, and he went
    Still in this fashion, colour, ornament,
    For him I imitate: O, if it prove,
    Tempests are kind and salt waves fresh in love!   [*Exit.*]
SIR TO. A very dishonest paltry boy, and more a coward than a hare:
    his dishonesty appears in leaving his friend here in necessity and
    denying him; and for his cowardship, ask Fabian.
FAB. A coward, a most devout coward, religious in it.
SIR AND. 'Slid,²⁵ I 'll after him again and beat him.
SIR TO. Do; cuff him soundly, but never draw thy sword.
SIR AND. An I do not,—   [*Exit.*]
FAB. Come, let 's see the event.
SIR TO. I dare lay any money 't will be nothing yet.   [*Exeunt.*]

ACT IV

SCENE I. *Before* OLIVIA'S *house.*

Enter SEBASTIAN *and* Clown

CLO. Will you make me believe that I am not sent for you?
SEB. Go to, go to, thou art a foolish fellow:
    Let me be clear of thee.
CLO. Well held out, i' faith! No, I do not know you; nor I am not sent
    to you by my lady, to bid you come speak with her; nor your name
    is not Master Cesario; nor this is not my nose neither. Nothing
    that is so is so.
SEB. I prithee, vent thy folly somewhere else:
    Thou know'st not me.
CLO. Vent my folly! he has heard that word of some great man and
    now applies it to a fool. Vent my folly! I am afraid this great lub-

---

25. *'Slid*] an oath, from "God's [eye]lid."

ber, the world, will prove a cockney.¹ I prithee now, ungird thy
strangeness and tell me what I shall vent to my lady: shall I vent to
her that thou art coming?

SEB.   I prithee, foolish Greek,² depart from me:
There 's money for thee: if you tarry longer,
I shall give worse payment.

CLO.   By my troth, thou hast an open hand. These wise men that give
fools money get themselves a good report—after fourteen years'
purchase.

Enter SIR ANDREW, SIR TOBY, *and* FABIAN

SIR AND.   Now, sir, have I met you again? there 's for you.

SEB.   Why, there 's for thee, and there, and there.
Are all the people mad?

SIR TO.   Hold, sir, or I 'll throw your dagger o'er the house.

CLO.   This will I tell my lady straight: I would not be in some of your
coats for two pence.   [*Exit.*]

SIR TO.   Come on, sir; hold.

SIR AND.   Nay, let him alone: I 'll go another way to work with him;
I 'll have an action of battery against him, if there be any law in
Illyria: though I struck him first, yet it 's no matter for that.

SEB.   Let go thy hand.

SIR TO.   Come, sir, I will not let you go. Come, my young soldier, put
up your iron: you are well fleshed; come on.

SEB.   I will be free from thee. What wouldst thou now?
If thou darest tempt me further, draw thy sword.

SIR TO.   What, what? Nay, then I must have an ounce or two of this
malapert blood from you.

Enter OLIVIA

OLI.   Hold, Toby; on thy life, I charge thee, hold!

SIR TO.   Madam!

OLI.   Will it be ever thus? Ungracious wretch,
Fit for the mountains and the barbarous caves,
Where manners ne'er were preach'd! out of my sight!
Be not offended, dear Cesario.
Rudesby,³ be gone! [*Exeunt* SIR TOBY, SIR ANDREW, *and* FABIAN.]
I prithee, gentle friend,

---

1. *cockney*] an effeminate fellow.
2. *Greek*] colloquial term for "fellow" or "companion."
3. *Rudesby*] boor.

Let thy fair wisdom, not thy passion, sway
In this uncivil and unjust extent
Against thy peace. Go with me to my house;
And hear thou there how many fruitless pranks
This ruffian hath botch'd up, that thou thereby
Mayst smile at this: thou shalt not choose but go:
Do not deny. Beshrew his soul for me,
He started one poor heart of mine in thee.

SEB.   What relish is in this? how runs the stream?
Or I am mad, or else this is a dream:
Let fancy still my sense in Lethe steep;
If it be thus to dream, still let me sleep!

OLI.   Nay, come, I prithee: would thou 'ldst be ruled by me!

SEB.   Madam, I will.

OLI.   O, say so, and so be!   [*Exeunt.*]

SCENE II. OLIVIA'S *house.*

Enter MARIA *and* Clown

MAR.   Nay, I prithee, put on this gown and this beard; make him
believe thou art Sir Topas the curate: do it quickly; I 'll call Sir
Toby the whilst.   [*Exit.*]

CLO.   Well, I 'll put it on, and I will dissemble myself in 't; and I
would I were the first that ever dissembled in such a gown. I am
not tall enough to become the function well, nor lean enough to
be thought a good student; but to be said an honest man and a
good housekeeper goes as fairly as to say a careful man and a great
scholar. The competitors enter.

Enter SIR TOBY *and* MARIA

SIR TO.   Jove bless thee, master Parson.

CLO.   Bonos dies, Sir Toby: for, as the old hermit of Prague, that never
saw pen and ink, very wittily said to a niece of King Gorboduc,[1]
"That that is is"; so I, being master Parson, am master Parson; for,
what is "that" but "that," and "is" but "is"?

_____
1. *Gorboduc*] a king of ancient Britain..

SIR TO. To him, Sir Topas.

CLO. What, ho, I say! peace in this prison!

SIR TO. The knave counterfeits well; a good knave.

MAL. [*within*] Who calls there?

CLO. Sir Topas the curate, who comes to visit Malvolio the lunatic.

MAL. Sir Topas, Sir Topas, good Sir Topas, go to my lady.

CLO. Out, hyperbolical fiend! how vexest thou this man! talkest thou nothing but of ladies?

SIR TO. Well said, master Parson.

MAL. Sir Topas, never was man thus wronged: good Sir Topas, do not think I am mad: they have laid me here in hideous darkness.

CLO. Fie, thou dishonest Satan! I call thee by the most modest terms; for I am one of those gentle ones that will use the devil himself with courtesy: sayest thou that house is dark?

MAL. As hell, Sir Topas.

CLO. Why, it hath bay windows transparent as barricadoes, and the clearstories[2] toward the south north are as lustrous as ebony; and yet complainest thou of obstruction?

MAL. I am not mad, Sir Topas: I say to you, this house is dark.

CLO. Madman, thou errest: I say, there is no darkness but ignorance; in which thou art more puzzled than the Egyptians in their fog.[3]

MAL. I say, this house is as dark as ignorance, though ignorance were as dark as hell; and I say, there was never man thus abused. I am no more mad than you are: make the trial of it any constant question.

CLO. What is the opinion of Pythagoras concerning wild fowl?

MAL. That the soul of our grandam might haply inhabit a bird.

CLO. What thinkest thou of his opinion?

MAL. I think nobly of the soul, and no way approve his opinion.

CLO. Fare thee well. Remain thou still in darkness: thou shalt hold the opinion of Pythagoras ere I will allow of thy wits; and fear to kill a woodcock, lest thou dispossess the soul of thy grandam. Fare thee well.

MAL. Sir Topas, Sir Topas!

SIR TO. My most exquisite Sir Topas!

CLO. Nay, I am for all waters.

MAR. Thou mightst have done this without thy beard and gown: he sees thee not.

---

2. *clearstories*] according to some sources, the upper row of windows on a house or church.

3. *Egyptians . . . fog*] One of the seven plagues inflicted upon the Egyptians as God's punishment of the Pharaoh for refusing to free the Hebrew slaves (see Exodus 10:21–23).

SIR TO. To him in thine own voice, and bring me word how thou
findest him: I would we were well rid of this knavery. If he may be
conveniently delivered, I would he were; for I am now so far in
offence with my niece, that I cannot pursue with any safety this
sport to the upshot. Come by and by to my chamber.

                          [*Exeunt* SIR TOBY *and* MARIA.]

CLO. [*Singing*] Hey, Robin, jolly Robin,
              Tell me how thy lady does.

MAL. Fool,—

CLO. My lady is unkind, perdy.[4]

MAL. Fool,—

CLO. Alas, why is she so?

MAL. Fool, I say,—

CLO. She loves another—Who calls, ha?

MAL. Good fool, as ever thou wilt deserve well at my hand, help me
to a candle, and pen, ink and paper: as I am a gentleman, I will
live to be thankful to thee for 't.

CLO. Master Malvolio!

MAL. Ay, good fool.

CLO. Alas, sir, how fell you besides your five wits?[5]

MAL. Fool, there was never man so notoriously abused: I am as well
in my wits, fool, as thou art.

CLO. But as well? then you are mad indeed, if you be no better in
your wits than a fool.

MAL. They have here propertied me;[6] keep me in darkness, send min-
isters to me, asses, and do all they can to face me out of my wits.

CLO. Advise you what you say; the minister is here. Malvolio,
Malvolio, thy wits the heavens restore! endeavour thyself to sleep,
and leave thy vain bibble babble.

MAL. Sir Topas,—

CLO. Maintain no words with him, good fellow. Who, I, sir? not I, sir.
God be wi' you, good Sir Topas. Marry, amen. I will, sir, I will.

MAL. Fool, fool, fool, I say,—

CLO. Alas, sir, be patient. What say you, sir? I am shent[7] for speaking
to you.

---

4. *perdy*] "by God" (from "par Dieu").

5. *five wits*] The "five wits" were common wit or intellectual power, imagination, fancy,
estimation and memory.

6. *propertied*] as a verb, to make property of, to make a tool, prop of.

7. *shent*] blamed, reproached.

MAL. Good fool, help me to some light and some paper: I tell thee, I
am as well in my wits as any man in Illyria.

CLO. Well-a-day that you were, sir!

MAL. By this hand, I am. Good fool, some ink, paper and light; and
convey what I will set down to my lady: it shall advantage thee
more than ever the bearing of letter did.

CLO. I will help you to 't. But tell me true, are you not mad indeed?
or do you but counterfeit?

MAL. Believe me, I am not; I tell thee true.

CLO. Nay, I 'll ne'er believe a madman till I see his brains. I will fetch
you light and paper and ink.

MAL. Fool, I 'll requite it in the highest degree: I prithee, be gone.

CLO. [*Singing*] I am gone, sir,
   And anon, sir,
  I 'll be with you again,
   In a trice,
   Like to the old vice,
 Your need to sustain;
 Who, with dagger of lath,[8]
 In his rage and his wrath,
  Cries, ah, ha! to the devil:
 Like a mad lad,
 Pare thy nails, dad;
  Adieu, goodman devil.   [*Exit.*]

SCENE III. OLIVIA'S *garden.*

Enter SEBASTIAN

SEB. This is the air; that is the glorious sun;
This pearl she gave me, I do feel 't and see 't;
And though 't is wonder that enwraps me thus,
Yet 't is not madness. Where 's Antonio, then?
I could not find him at the Elephant:
Yet there he was; and there I found this credit,[1]

---

8. *lath*] a piece of wood.

---

1. *credit*] belief or opinion.

That he did range the town to seek me out.
His counsel now might do me golden service;
For though my soul disputes well with my sense,
That this may be some error, but no madness,
Yet doth this accident and flood of fortune
So far exceed all instance, all discourse,
That I am ready to distrust mine eyes
And wrangle with my reason, that persuades me
To any other trust but that I am mad,
Or else the lady 's mad; yet, if 't were so,
She could not sway her house, command her followers,
Take and give back affairs and their dispatch
With such a smooth, discreet, and stable bearing
As I perceive she does: there 's something in 't
That is deceivable. But here the lady comes.

Enter OLIVIA *and* Priest

OLI. Blame not this haste of mine. If you mean well,
Now go with me and with this holy man
Into the chantry by: there, before him,
And underneath that consecrated roof,
Plight me the full assurance of your faith;
That my most jealous and too doubtful soul
May live at peace. He shall conceal it
Whiles you are willing it shall come to note,
What time we will our celebration keep
According to my birth. What do you say?
SEB. I 'll follow this good man, and go with you;
And, having sworn truth, ever will be true.
OLI. Then lead the way, good father; and heavens so shine,
That they may fairly note this act of mine!   [*Exeunt.*]

ACT V

SCENE I. *Before* OLIVIA'S *house.*

Enter Clown *and* FABIAN

FAB.   Now, as thou lovest me, let me see his letter.

CLO.   Good Master Fabian, grant me another request.

FAB.   Any thing.

CLO.   Do not desire to see this letter.

FAB.   This is, to give a dog, and in recompense desire my dog again.

Enter DUKE, VIOLA, CURIO, *and* Lords

DUKE.   Belong you to the Lady Olivia, friends?

CLO.   Ay, sir; we are some of her trappings.

DUKE.   I know thee well: how dost thou, my good fellow?

CLO.   Truly, sir, the better for my foes and the worse for my friends.

DUKE.   Just the contrary; the better for thy friends.

CLO.   No, sir, the worse.

DUKE.   How can that be?

CLO.   Marry, sir, they praise me and make an ass of me; now my foes
tell me plainly I am an ass: so that by my foes, sir, I profit in the
knowledge of myself; and by my friends I am abused: so that, con-
clusions to be as kisses, if your four negatives make your two affir-
matives, why then, the worse for my friends, and the better for my
foes.

DUKE.   Why, this is excellent.

CLO.   By my troth, sir, no; though it please you to be one of my
friends.

DUKE.   Thou shalt not be the worse for me: there 's gold.

CLO.   But that it would be double-dealing, sir, I would you could
make it another.

DUKE.   O, you give me ill counsel.

CLO.   Put your grace in your pocket, sir, for this once, and let your
flesh and blood obey it.

DUKE.   Well, I will be so much a sinner, to be a double-dealer: there's
another.

CLO.   Primo, secundo, tertio, is a good play; and the old saying is, the

third pays for all: the triplex, sir, is a good tripping measure; or the
bells of Saint Bennet,[1] sir, may put you in mind; one, two, three.

DUKE.   You can fool no more money out of me at this throw: if you
will let your lady know I am here to speak with her, and bring her
along with you, it may awake my bounty further.

CLO.   Marry, sir, lullaby to your bounty till I come again. I go, sir; but
I would not have you to think that my desire of having is the sin
of covetousness: but, as you say, sir, let your bounty take a nap, I
will awake it anon.   [*Exit.*]

VIO.   Here comes the man, sir, that did rescue me.

Enter ANTONIO *and* Officers

DUKE.   That face of his I do remember well;
Yet, when I saw it last, it was besmear'd
As black as Vulcan[2] in the smoke of war:
A bawbling[3] vessel was he captain of,
For shallow draught and bulk unprizable;[4]
With which such scathful grapple did he make
With the most noble bottom of our fleet,
That very envy and the tongue of loss
Cried fame and honour on him.[5] What 's the matter?

FIRST OFF.   Orsino, this is that Antonio
That took the Phœnix and her fraught[6] from Candy;[7]
And this is he that did the Tiger board,
When your young nephew Titus lost his leg:
Here in the streets, desperate of shame and state,[8]
In private brabble did we apprehend him.

VIO.   He did me kindness, sir, drew on my side;
But in conclusion put strange speech upon me:
I know not what 't was but distraction.

---

1. *bells of Saint Bennet*] a reference to the chimes sounded by the bells of St. Bennet's
Church on Paul's Wharf, which was destroyed in the great fire of London.
2. *Vulcan*] the Roman god of fire and metalsmithing, usually portrayed with skin black-
ened from the smoke of his forge
3. *bawbling*] trifling, of small value.
4. *unprizable*] without value as a prize of war.
5. *scathful grapple . . . on him*] He grappled with such destructive violence with the finest
ship of our fleet that those who had best right to hate him and loudly lamented their
loss, extolled him.
6. *fraught*] freight, cargo.
7. *Candy*] the island of Crete, at that time called Candia.
8. *desperate . . . state*] reckless of disgrace and oblivious of his rank.

DUKE.   Notable pirate! thou salt-water thief!
　　 What foolish boldness brought thee to their mercies,
　　 Whom thou, in terms so bloody and so dear,
　　 Hast made thine enemies?
ANT. 　　　　　　　　　 Orsino, noble sir,
　　 Be pleased that I shake off these names you give me:
　　 Antonio never yet was thief or pirate,
　　 Though I confess, on base and ground enough,
　　 Orsino's enemy. A witchcraft drew me hither:
　　 That most ingrateful boy there by your side,
　　 From the rude sea's enraged and foamy mouth
　　 Did I redeem; a wreck past hope he was:
　　 His life I gave him and did thereto add
　　 My love, without retention or restraint,
　　 All his in dedication; for his sake
　　 Did I expose myself, pure[9] for his love,
　　 Into the danger of this adverse town;
　　 Drew to defend him when he was beset:
　　 Where being apprehended, his false cunning,
　　 Not meaning to partake with me in danger,
　　 Taught him to face me out of his acquaintance,[10]
　　 And grew a twenty years removed thing
　　 While one would wink; denied me mine own purse,
　　 Which I had recommended to his use
　　 Not half an hour before.
VIO. 　　　　　　　　　 How can this be?
DUKE.   When came he to this town?
ANT.   To-day, my lord; and for three months before,
　　 No interim, not a minute's vacancy,
　　 Both day and night did we keep company.

Enter OLIVIA *and* Attendants

DUKE.   Here comes the countess: now heaven walks on earth.
　　 But for thee, fellow; fellow, thy words are madness:
　　 Three months this youth hath tended upon me;
　　 But more of that anon. Take him aside.
OLI.   What would my lord, but that he may not have,
　　 Wherein Olivia may seem serviceable?

---

9. *pure*] the adjective used adverbially, "purely," "solely."
10. *face me . . . acquaintance*] brazenly deny knowledge of me.

Cesario, you do not keep promise with me.

VIO. Madam!

DUKE. Gracious Olivia,—

OLI. What do you say, Cesario? Good my lord,—

VIO. My lord would speak; my duty hushes me.

OLI. If it be aught to the old tune, my lord,

It is as fat and fulsome[11] to mine ear

As howling after music.

DUKE.   Still so cruel?

OLI. Still so constant, lord.

DUKE. What, to perverseness? you uncivil lady,

To whose ingrate and unauspicious altars

My soul the faithfull'st offerings hath breathed out

That e'er devotion tender'd! What shall I do?

OLI. Even what it please my lord, that shall become him.

DUKE. Why should I not, had I the heart to do it,

Like to the Egyptian thief at point of death,

Kill what I love?—[12]a savage jealousy

That sometimes savours nobly. But hear me this:

Since you to non-regardance cast my faith,

And that I partly know the instrument

That screws me from my true place in your favour,

Live you the marble-breasted tyrant still;

But this your minion, whom I know you love,

And whom, by heaven I swear, I tender dearly,

Him will I tear out of that cruel eye,

Where he sits crowned in his master's spite.

Come, boy, with me; my thoughts are ripe in mischief:

I 'll sacrifice the lamb that I do love,

To spite a raven's heart within a dove.

VIO. And I, most jocund, apt and willing,

To do you rest, a thousand deaths would die.

OLI. Where goes Cesario?

VIO.   After him I love

More than I love these eyes, more than my life,

More, by all mores, than e'er I shall love wife.

---

11. *fat and fulsome*] nauseous and cloying.

12. *the Egyptian thief . . . love?*] A reference to the story of Theagenes and Chariclea in Heliodorus, *Æthiopica* (translated by Thomas Underdowne, 1569), where Thyamis, an Egyptian thief, slays a captive whom he mistakes for the object of his affection, in the fear that he is about to be robbed of her.

If I do feign, you witnesses above
Punish my life for tainting of my love!
OLI.   Ay me, detested! how am I beguiled!
VIO.   Who does beguile you? who does do you wrong?
OLI.   Hast thou forgot thyself? is it so long?
Call forth the holy father.
DUKE.   Come, away!
OLI.   Whither, my lord? Cesario, husband, stay.
DUKE.   Husband!
OLI.   Ay, husband: can he that deny?
DUKE.   Her husband, sirrah!
VIO.   No, my lord, not I.
OLI.   Alas, it is the baseness of thy fear
That makes thee strangle thy propriety:[13]
Fear not, Cesario; take thy fortunes up;
Be that thou know'st thou art, and then thou art
As great as that thou fear'st.

Enter Priest

                        O, welcome, father!
Father, I charge thee, by thy reverence,
Here to unfold, though lately we intended
To keep in darkness what occasion now
Reveals before 't is ripe, what thou dost know
Hath newly pass'd between this youth and me.
PRIEST.   A contract of eternal bond of love,[14]
Confirm'd by mutual joinder of your hands,
Attested by the holy close of lips,
Strengthen'd by interchangement of your rings;
And all the ceremony of this compact
Seal'd in my function,[15] by my testimony:
Since when, my watch hath told me, toward my grave
I have travell'd but two hours.
DUKE.   O thou dissembling cub! what wilt thou be
When time hath sow'd a grizzle on thy case?[16]
Or will not else thy craft so quickly grow,

13. *propriety*] identity or individuality.
14. A *contract . . . love*] the ordinary ceremony of a betrothal, which preceeded the marriage rite.
15. *function*] office as chaplain to Olivia.
16. *a grizzle on thy case*] a touch of grey on thy skin.

That thine own trip shall be thine overthrow?
Farewell, and take her; but direct thy feet
Where thou and I henceforth may never meet.

VIO.   My lord, I do protest—

OLI.   O, do not swear!
Hold little faith, though thou hast too much fear.

Enter SIR ANDREW

SIR AND.   For the love of God, a surgeon! Send one presently to Sir
     Toby.

OLI.   What 's the matter?

SIR AND.   He has broke my head across and has given Sir Toby a
     bloody coxcomb too: for the love of God, your help! I had rather
     than forty pound I were at home.

OLI.   Who has done this, Sir Andrew?

SIR AND.   The count's gentleman, one Cesario: we took him for a
     coward, but he 's the very devil incardinate.

DUKE.   My gentleman, Cesario?

SIR AND.   'Od's lifelings, here he is! You broke my head for nothing;
     and that that I did, I was set on to do 't by Sir Toby.

VIO.   Why do you speak to me? I never hurt you:
You drew your sword upon me without cause;
But I bespake you fair, and hurt you not.

SIR AND.   If a bloody coxcomb be a hurt, you have hurt me: I think
     you set nothing by a bloody coxcomb.

Enter SIR TOBY *and* Clown

Here comes Sir Toby halting; you shall hear more: but if he had
     not been in drink, he would have tickled you othergates[17] than he
     did.

DUKE.   How now, gentleman! how is 't with you?

SIR TO.   That 's all one: has hurt me, and there 's the end on 't. Sot,
     didst see Dick surgeon, sot?

CLO.   O, he 's drunk, Sir Toby, an hour agone; his eyes were set at
     eight i' the morning.

SIR TO.   Then he 's a rogue, and a passy measures pavin:[18] I hate a
     drunken rogue.

---

17. *othergates*] Sir Andrew's word for otherwise, in another manner.

18. *passy measures pavin*] "Pavin" is the name of a stately dance, and "passy measures" is
     a corruption of "passamezzo," a slow and solemn step which formed chief part of the
     "pavin."

OLI.   Away with him! Who hath made this havoc with them?

SIR AND.   I 'll help you, Sir Toby, because we 'll be dressed together.

SIR TO.   Will you help? an ass-head and a coxcomb and a knave, a
      thin-faced knave, a gull!

OLI.   Get him to bed, and let his hurt be look'd to.

> [*Exeunt* Clown, FABIAN, SIR TOBY, *and* SIR ANDREW.]

Enter SEBASTIAN

SEB.   I am sorry, madam, I have hurt your kinsman;
      But, had it been the brother of my blood,
      I must have done no less with wit and safety.
      You throw a strange regard[19] upon me, and by that
      I do perceive it hath offended you:
      Pardon me, sweet one, even for the vows
      We made each other but so late ago.

DUKE.   One face, one voice, one habit, and two persons,
      A natural perspective,[20] that is and is not!

SEB.   Antonio, O my dear Antonio!
      How have the hours rack'd and tortured me,
      Since I have lost thee!

ANT.   Sebastian are you?

SEB.   Fear'st thou that, Antonio?

ANT.   How have you made division of yourself?
      An apple, cleft in two, is not more twin
      Than these two creatures.Which is Sebastian?

OLI.   Most wonderful!

SEB.   Do I stand there? I never had a brother;
      Nor can there be that deity in my nature,
      Of here and every where. I had a sister,
      Whom the blind waves and surges have devour'd.
      Of charity, what kin are you to me?
      What countryman? what name? what parentage?

VIO.   Of Messaline: Sebastian was my father;
      Such a Sebastian was my brother too,
      So went he suited[21] to his watery tomb:
      If spirits can assume both form and suit,
      You come to fright us.

---

19. *regard*] look.

20. *perspective*] an ingeniously contrived glass, which was capable of producing the optical delusion of making one person look like two.

21. *suited*] in such a suit of clothes.

SEB.   A spirit I am indeed;
    But am in that dimension grossly clad
    Which from the womb I did participate.
    Were you a woman, as the rest goes even,
    I should my tears let fall upon your cheek,
    And say, "Thrice-welcome, drowned Viola!"
VIO.   My father had a mole upon his brow.
SEB.   And so had mine.
VIO.   And died that day when Viola from her birth
    Had number'd thirteen years.
SEB.   O, that record is lively in my soul!
    He finished indeed his mortal act
    That day that made my sister thirteen years.
VIO.   If nothing lets[22] to make us happy both
    But this my masculine usurp'd attire,
    Do not embrace me till each circumstance
    Of place, time, fortune, do cohere and jump
    That I am Viola: which to confirm,
    I 'll bring you to a captain in this town,
    Where lie my maiden weeds; by whose gentle help
    I was preserved to serve this noble count.
    All the occurrence of my fortune since
    Hath been between this lady and this lord.
SEB.   [To OLIVIA] So comes it, lady, you have been mistook:
    But nature to her bias drew in that.
    You would have been contracted to a maid;
    Nor are you therein, by my life, deceived,
    You are betroth'd both to a maid and man.
DUKE.   Be not amazed; right noble is his blood.
    If this be so, as yet the glass seems true,
    I shall have share in this most happy wreck.
    [To VIOLA] Boy, thou hast said to me a thousand times
    Thou never shouldst love woman like to me.
VIO.   And all those sayings will I over-swear;
    And all those swearings keep as true in soul
    As doth that orbed continent the fire
    That severs day from night.
DUKE.   Give me thy hand;
    And let me see thee in thy woman's weeds.

---

22. *lets*] prevents.

VIO. The captain that did bring me first on shore
　　　Hath my maid's garments: he upon some action
　　　Is now in durance, at Malvolio's suit,
　　　A gentleman, and follower of my lady's.
OLI. He shall enlarge him: fetch Malvolio hither:
　　　And yet, alas, now I remember me,
　　　They say, poor gentleman, he 's much distract.

Re-enter Clown *with a letter, and* FABIAN

　　　A most extracting frenzy of mine own
　　　From my remembrance clearly banish'd his.
　　　How does he, sirrah?
CLO. Truly, madam, he holds Belzebub at the stave's end as well as a
　　　man in his case may do: has here writ a letter to you; I should have
　　　given 't you to-day morning, but as a madman's epistles are no
　　　gospels, so it skills not much when they are delivered.
OLI. Open 't, and read it.
CLO. Look then to be well edified when the fool delivers the mad-
　　　man. [*Reads*] By the Lord, madam,—
OLI. How now! art thou mad?
CLO. No, madam, I do but read madness: an your ladyship will have
　　　it as it ought to be, you must allow Vox.[23]
OLI. Prithee, read i' thy right wits.
CLO. So I do, madonna; but to read his right wits is to read thus:
　　　therefore perpend,[24] my princess, and give ear.
OLI. Read it you, sirrah. [*To* FABIAN.]
FAB. [*Reads*] By the Lord, madam, you wrong me, and the world shall know
　　　it: though you have put me into darkness and given your drunken cousin
　　　rule over me, yet have I the benefit of my senses as well as your ladyship.
　　　I have your own letter that induced me to the semblance I put on; with
　　　the which I doubt not but to do myself much right, or you much shame.
　　　Think of me as you please. I leave my duty a little unthought of, and
　　　speak out of my injury.

　　　　　　　　　　　　　　　　　THE MADLY-USED MALVOLIO.
OLI. Did he write this?
CLO. Ay, madam.
DUKE. This savours not much of distraction.
OLI. See him deliver'd, Fabian; bring him hither. [*Exit* FABIAN.]
　　　My lord, so please you, these things further thought on,

---

23. *allow Vox*] allow me the use of my voice.
24. *perpend*] consider.

To think me as well a sister as a wife,
One day shall crown the alliance on 't, so please you,
Here at my house and at my proper cost.

DUKE.   Madam, I am most apt to embrace your offer.
[*To* VIOLA] Your master quits you; and for your service done him,
So much against the mettle of your sex,
So far beneath your soft and tender breeding,
And since you call'd me master for so long,
Here is my hand: you shall from this time be
Your master's mistress.

OLI.   A sister! you are she.

Re-enter FABIAN, *with* MALVOLIO

DUKE.   Is this the madman?
OLI.   Ay, my lord, this same.
How now, Malvolio!
MAL.   Madam, you have done me wrong,
Notorious wrong.
OLI.   Have I, Malvolio? no.
MAL.   Lady, you have. Pray you, peruse that letter.
You must not now deny it is your hand:
Write from it,[25] if you can, in hand or phrase;
Or say 't is not your seal, not your invention:
You can say none of this: well, grant it then
And tell me, in the modesty of honour,
Why you have given me such clear lights of favour,
Bade me come smiling and cross-garter'd to you,
To put on yellow stockings and to frown
Upon Sir Toby and the lighter people;
And, acting this in an obedient hope,
Why have you suffer'd me to be imprison'd,
Kept in a dark house, visited by the priest,
And made the most notorious geck[26] and gull
That e'er invention play'd on? tell my why.
OLI.   Alas, Malvolio, this is not my writing,
Though, I confess, much like the character:
But out of question 't is Maria's hand.
And now I do bethink me, it was she

---

25. *Write from it*] Write differently from it.
26. *geck*] dupe.

First told me thou wast mad; then camest in smiling,
And in such forms which here were presupposed
Upon thee in the letter. Prithee, be content:
This practice hath most shrewdly pass'd upon thee;
But when we know the grounds and authors of it,
Thou shalt be both the plaintiff and the judge
Of thine own cause.

FAB.   Good madam, hear me speak,
And let no quarrel nor no brawl to come
Taint the condition of this present hour,
Which I have wonder'd at. In hope it shall not,
Most freely I confess, myself and Toby
Set this device against Malvolio here,
Upon some stubborn and uncourteous parts
We had conceived against him: Maria writ
The letter at Sir Toby's great importance;[27]
In recompense whereof he hath married her.
How with a sportful malice it was follow'd
May rather pluck on laughter than revenge;
If that the injuries be justly weigh'd
That have on both sides pass'd.

OLI.   Alas, poor fool, how have they baffled thee!

CLO.   Why, "some are born great, some achieve greatness, and some
have greatness thrown upon them." I was one, sir, in this interlude; one Sir Topas, sir; but that's all one. "By the Lord, fool, I am
not mad." But do you remember? "Madam, why laugh you at such
a barren rascal? an you smile not, he's gagged": and thus the
whirligig of time brings in his revenges.

MAL.   I'll be revenged on the whole pack of you.   [*Exit.*]

OLI.   He hath been most notoriously abused.

DUKE.   Pursue him, and entreat him to a peace:
He hath not told us of the captain yet:
When that is known, and golden time convents,[28]
A solemn combination shall be made
Of our dear souls. Meantime, sweet sister,
We will not part from hence. Cesario, come;
For so you shall be, while you are a man;
But when in other habits you are seen,

---

27. *importance*] insistent request.
28. *convents*] suits.

Orsino's mistress and his fancy's queen.

[*Exeunt all, except* Clown.]

CLO.   [*Sings*]

> When that I was and a little tiny boy,
>   With hey, ho, the wind and the rain,
> A foolish thing was but a toy,
>   For the rain it raineth every day.
>
> But when I came to man's estate,
>   With hey, ho, &c.
> 'Gainst knaves and thieves men shut their gate,
>   For the rain, &c.
>
> But when I came, alas! to wive,
>   With hey, ho, &c.
> By swaggering could I never thrive,
>   For the rain, &c.
>
> But when I came unto my beds,
>   With hey, ho, &c.
> With toss-pots still had drunken heads,
>   For the rain, &c.
>
> A great while ago the world begun,
>   With hey, ho, &c.
> But that's all one, our play is done,
>   And we 'll strive to please you every day.   [*Exit.*]

Study Guide

Text by
Frederic Kolman
(M.A., Rutgers University)

Foreign Language Department
Louis D. Brandeis High School
New York, New York

Contents

Section One: *Introduction* 77

   The Life and Work of William Shakespeare 77

   Shakesperian Language 79

   Historical Background 92

   Master List of Characters 93

   Summary of the Play 94

   Estimated Reading Time 95

**Each scene includes List of Characters,
Summary, Analysis, Study Questions and
Answers, and Suggested Essay Topics.**

Section Two: *Act I* 96

   Scene I 96

   Scene II 100

   Scene III 103

Scene IV 106

Scene V 109

Section Three: *Act II* 113

Scene I 113

Scene II 116

Scene III 119

Scene IV 122

Scene V 125

Section Four: *Act III* 130

Scene I 130

Scene II 134

Scene III 137

Scene IV 139

Section Five: *Act IV* 145

Scene I 145

Scene II 148

Scene III 152

Section Six: *Act V* 155

Scene I 155

Section Seven: *Bibliography* 161

SECTION ONE

Introduction

The Life and Work of William Shakespeare

The details of William Shakespeare's life are sketchy, mostly mere surmise based upon court or other clerical records. His parents, John and Mary (Arden), were married about 1557; she was of the landed gentry, and he was a yeoman—a glover and commodities merchant. By 1568, John had risen through the ranks of town government and held the position of high bailiff, which was a position similar to mayor. William, the eldest son and the third of eight children, was born in 1564, probably on April 23, several days before his baptism on April 26 in Stratford-upon-Avon. Shakespeare is also believed to have died on the same date—April 23—in 1616.

It is believed that William attended the local grammar school in Stratford where his parents lived, and that he studied primarily Latin, rhetoric, logic, and literature. Shakespeare probably left school at age 15, which was the norm, to take a job, especially since this was the period of his father's financial difficulty. At age 18 (1582), William married Anne Hathaway, a local farmer's daughter who was eight years his senior. Their first daughter (Susanna) was born six months later (1583), and twins Judith and Hamnet were born in 1585.

Shakespeare's life can be divided into three periods: the first 20 years in Stratford, which include his schooling, early marriage, and fatherhood; the next 25 years as an actor and playwright in London; and the last five in retirement in Stratford where he enjoyed moderate wealth gained from his theatrical successes. The years linking the first two periods are marked by a lack of information about Shakespeare, and are often referred to as the "dark years."

At some point during the "dark years," Shakespeare began his career with a London theatrical company, perhaps in 1589, for he was already an actor and playwright of some note by 1592. Shakespeare apparently wrote and acted for numerous theatrical companies, including Pembroke's Men, and Strange's Men, which later became the Chamberlain's Men, with whom he remained for the rest of his career.

In 1592, the Plague closed the theaters for about two years, and Shakespeare turned to writing book-length narrative poetry. Most notable were *Venus and Adonis* and *The Rape of Lucrece*, both of which were dedicated to the Earl of Southampton, whom scholars accept as Shakespeare's friend and benefactor despite a lack of documentation. During this same period, Shakespeare was writing his sonnets, which are more likely signs of the time's fashion rather than actual love poems detailing any particular relationship. He returned to playwriting when theaters reopened in 1594, and did not continue to write poetry. His sonnets were published without his consent in 1609, shortly before his retirement.

Amid all of his success, Shakespeare suffered the loss of his only son, Hamnet, who died in 1596 at the age of 11. But Shakespeare's career continued unabated, and in London in 1599, he became one of the partners in the new Globe Theater, which was built by the Chamberlain's Men.

Shakespeare wrote very little after 1612, which was the year he completed *Henry VIII*. It was during a performance of this play in 1613 that the Globe caught fire and burned to the ground. Sometime between 1610 and 1613, Shakespeare returned to Stratford, where he owned a large house and property, to spend his remaining years with his family.

William Shakespeare died on April 23, 1616, and was buried two days later in the chancel of Holy Trinity Church, where he had been baptized exactly 52 years earlier. His literary legacy included 37 plays, 154 sonnets, and five major poems.

Incredibly, most of Shakespeare's plays had never been published in anything except pamphlet form, and were simply extant as acting scripts stored at the Globe. Theater scripts were not regarded as literary works of art, but only the basis for the performance. Plays were simply a popular form of entertainment for all layers of society in Shakespeare's time. Only the efforts of two of Shakespeare's company, John Heminges and Henry Condell, preserved his 36 plays (minus *Pericles*, the thirty-seventh).

Shakespeare's Language

Shakespeare's language can create a strong pang of intimidation, even fear, in a large number of modern-day readers. Fortunately, however, this need not be the case. All that is needed to master the art of reading Shakespeare is to practice the techniques of unraveling uncommonly-structured sentences and to become familiar with the poetic use of uncommon words. We must realize that during the 400-year span between Shakespeare's time and our own, both the way we live and speak has changed. Although most of his vocabulary is in use today, some of it is obsolete, and what may be most confusing is that some of his words are used today, but with slightly different or totally different meanings. On the stage, actors readily dissolve these language stumbling blocks. They study Shakespeare's dialogue and express it dramatically in word and in action so that its meaning is graphically enacted. If the reader studies Shakespeare's lines as an actor does, looking up and reflecting upon the meaning of unfamiliar words until real voice is discovered, he or she will suddenly experience the excitement, the depth and the sheer poetry of what these characters say.

Shakespeare's Sentences

In English, or any other language, the meaning of a sentence greatly depends upon where each word is placed in that sentence. "The child hurt the mother" and "The mother hurt the child" have opposite meanings, even though the words are the same, simply because the words are arranged differently. Because word position is so integral to English, the reader will find unfamiliar word arrangements confusing, even difficult to understand. Since Shakespeare's plays are poetic dramas, he often shifts from average word arrangements to the strikingly unusual so that the line will conform to the desired poetic rhythm. Often, too, Shakespeare employs unusual word order to afford a character his own specific style of speaking.

Today, English sentence structure follows a sequence of subject first, verb second, and an optional object third. Shakespeare, however, often places the verb before the subject, which reads, "Speaks he" rather than "He speaks." Solanio speaks with this inverted structure in *The Merchant of Venice* stating, "I should be still/Plucking the grass to know where sits the wind" (Bevington edition, I, i, ll.17-19), while today's standard English word order would have the clause at the end of this line read, "where the wind sits." "Wind" is the subject of this clause, and "sits" is the verb. Bassanio's words in Act Two also exemplify this inversion: "And in such eyes as ours appear not faults" (II, ii, l. 184). In our normal word order, we would say, "Faults do not appear in eyes such as ours," with "faults" as the subject in both Shakespeare's word order and ours.

Inversions like these are not troublesome, but when Shakespeare positions the predicate adjective or the object before the subject and verb, we are sometimes surprised. For example, rather than "I saw him," Shakespeare may use a structure such as "Him I saw." Similarly, "Cold the morning is" would be used for our "The morning is cold." Lady Macbeth demonstrates this inversion as she speaks of her husband: "Glamis thou art, and Cawdor, and shalt be/What thou art promised" (Macbeth, I, v, ll. 14-15). In current English word order, this quote would begin, "Thou art Glamis, and Cawdor."

In addition to inversions, Shakespeare purposefully keeps words apart that we generally keep together. To illustrate, consider Bassanio's humble admission in *The Merchant of Venice*: "I owe you much, and, like a wilful youth,/That which I owe is lost" (I, i, ll. 146-147). The phrase, "like a wilful youth," separates the regular sequence of "I owe you much" and "That which I owe is lost." To understand more clearly this type of passage, the reader could rearrange these word groups into our conventional order: I owe you much and I wasted what you gave me because I was young and impulsive. While these rearranged clauses will sound like normal English, and will be simpler to understand, they will no longer have the desired poetic rhythm, and the emphasis will now be on the wrong words.

As we read Shakespeare, we will find words that are separated by long, interruptive statements. Often subjects are separated from verbs, and verbs are separated from objects. These long interruptions can be used to give a character dimension or to add an element of suspense. For example, in *Romeo and Juliet* Benvolio describes both Romeo's moodiness and his own sensitive and thoughtful nature:

> I, measuring his affections by my own,
> Which then most sought, where most might not be
> found,
> Being one too many by my weary self,
> Pursu'd my humour, not pursuing his,
> And gladly shunn'd who gladly fled from me.
> (I, i, ll. 126-130)

In this passage, the subject "I" is distanced from its verb "Pursu'd." The long interruption serves to provide information which is integral to the plot. Another example, taken from *Hamlet*, is the ghost, Hamlet's father, who describes Hamlet's uncle, Claudius, as

> ...that incestuous, that adulterate beast,
> With witchcraft of his wit, with traitorous gifts—
> O wicked wit and gifts, that have the power
> So to seduce—won to his shameful lust
> The will of my most seeming virtuous queen. (I, v, ll. 43-47)

From this we learn that Prince Hamlet's mother is the victim of an evil seduction and deception. The delay between the subject, "beast," and the verb, "won," creates a moment of tension filled with the image of a cunning predator waiting for the right moment to spring into attack. This interruptive passage allows the play to unfold crucial information and thus to build the tension necessary to produce a riveting drama.

While at times these long delays are merely for decorative purposes, they are often used to narrate a particular situation or to enhance character development. As *Antony and Cleopatra* opens, an interruptive passage occurs in the first few lines. Although the delay is not lengthy, Philo's words vividly portray Antony's military prowess while they also reveal the immediate concern of the drama. Antony is distracted from his career, and is now focused on Cleopatra:

> ...those goodly eyes,
> That o'er the files and musters of the war
> Have glow'd like plated Mars, now bend, now turn
> The office and devotion of their view
> Upon a tawny front.... (I, i, ll. 2-6)

Whereas Shakespeare sometimes heaps detail upon detail, his sentences are often elliptical, that is, they omit words we expect in written English sentences. In fact, we often do this in our spoken conversations. For instance, we say, "You see that?" when we really mean, "Did you see that?" Reading poetry or listening to lyrics in music conditions us to supply the omitted words and it makes us more comfortable reading this type of dialogue. Consider one passage in *The Merchant of Venice* where Antonio's friends ask him why he seems so sad and Solanio tells Antonio, "Why, then you are in love" (I, i, l. 46). When Antonio denies this, Solanio responds, "Not in love neither?" (I, i, l. 47). The word "you" is omitted but understood despite the confusing double negative.

In addition to leaving out words, Shakespeare often uses intentionally vague language, a strategy which taxes the reader's attentiveness. In *Antony and Cleopatra*, Cleopatra, upset that Antony is leaving for Rome after learning that his wife died in battle, convinces him to stay in Egypt:

> Sir, you and I must part, but that's not it:
> Sir you and I have lov'd, but there's not it;
> That you know well, something it is I would—
> O, my oblivion is a very Antony,
> And I am all forgotten. (I, iii, ll. 87-91, emphasis added)

In line 89, "...something it is I would" suggests that there is something that she would want to say, do, or have done. The intentional vagueness leaves us, and certainly Antony, to wonder. Though this sort of writing may appear lackadaisical for all that it leaves out, here the vagueness functions to portray Cleopatra as rhetorically sophisticated. Similarly, when asked what thing a crocodile is (meaning Antony himself who is being compared to a crocodile), Antony slyly evades the question by giving a vague reply:

> It is shap'd, sir, like itself, and it is as broad as it hath breadth. It is just so high as it is, and moves with it own organs. It lives by that which nourisheth it, and, the elements once out of it, it transmigrates. (II, vii, ll. 43-46)

This kind of evasiveness, or doubletalk, occurs often in Shakespeare's writing and requires extra patience on the part of the reader.

Shakespeare's Words

As we read Shakespeare's plays, we will encounter uncommon words. Many of these words are not in use today. As *Romeo and Juliet* opens, we notice words like "shrift" (confession) and "holidame" (a holy relic). Words like these should be explained in notes to the text. Shakespeare also employs words which we still use, though with different meaning. For example, in *The Merchant of Venice* "caskets" refer to small, decorative chests for holding jewels. However, modern readers may think of a large cask instead of the smaller, diminutive casket.

Another trouble modern readers will have with Shakespeare's English is with words that are still in use today, but which mean something different in Elizabethan use. In *The Merchant of Venice*, Shakespeare uses the word "straight" (as in "straight away") where we would say "immediately." Here, the modern reader is unlikely to carry away the wrong message, however, since the modern meaning will simply make no sense. In this case, textual notes will clarify a phrase's meaning. To cite another example, in *Romeo and Juliet*, after Mercutio dies, Romeo states that the "black fate on moe days doth depend" (emphasis added). In this case, "depend" really means "impend."

Shakespeare's Wordplay

All of Shakespeare's works exhibit his mastery of playing with language and with such variety that many people have authored entire books on this subject alone. Shakespeare's most frequently used types of wordplay are common: metaphors, similes, synecdoche and metonymy, personification, allusion, and puns. It is when Shakespeare violates the normal use of these devices, or rhetorical figures, that the language becomes confusing.

A metaphor is a comparison in which an object or idea is replaced by another object or idea with common attributes. For example, in *Macbeth* a murderer tells Macbeth that Banquo has been murdered, as directed, but that his son, Fleance, escaped, having witnessed his father's murder. Fleance, now a threat to Macbeth, is described as a serpent:

> There the grown serpent lies, the worm that's fled
> Hath nature that in time will venom breed,
> No teeth for the present. (III, iv, ll. 29-31)

Similes, on the other hand, compare objects or ideas while using the words "like" or "as." In *Romeo and Juliet*, Romeo tells Juliet that "Love goes toward love as schoolboys from their books" (II, ii, l. 156). Such similes often give way to more involved comparisons, "extended similes." For example, Juliet tells Romeo:

> 'Tis almost morning, I would have thee gone,
> And yet no farther than a wonton's bird,
> That lets it hop a little from his hand
> Like a poor prisoner in his twisted gyves,
> And with silken thread plucks it back again,
> So loving-jealous of his liberty.
> (II, ii, ll. 176-181)

An epic simile, a device borrowed from heroic poetry, is an extended simile that builds into an even more elaborate comparison. In *Macbeth*, Macbeth describes King Duncan's virtues with an angelic, celestial simile and then drives immediately into another simile that redirects us into a vision of warfare and destruction:

> ...Besides this Duncan
> Hath borne his faculties so meek, hath been
> So clear in his great office, that his virtues
> Will plead like angels, trumpet-tongued, against
> The deep damnation of his taking-off;
> And pity, like a naked new-born babe,

Striding the blast, or heaven's cherubim, horsed
Upon the sightless couriers of the air,
Shall blow the horrid deed in every eye,
That tears shall drown the wind....
(I, vii, ll. 16-25)

Shakespeare employs other devices, like synecdoche and metonymy, to achieve "verbal economy," or using one or two words to express more than one thought. Synecdoche is a figure of speech using a part for the whole. An example of synecdoche is using the word boards to imply a stage. Boards are only a small part of the materials that make up a stage, however, the term boards has become a colloquial synonym for stage. Metonymy is a figure of speech using the name of one thing for that of another which it is associated. An example of metonymy is using crown to mean the king (as used in the sentence "These lands belong to the crown"). Since a crown is associated with or an attribute of the king, the word crown has become a metonymy for the king. It is important to understand that every metonymy is a synecdoche, but not every synecdoche is a metonymy. This is rule is true because a metonymy must not only be a part of the root word, making a synecdoche, but also be a unique attribute of or associated with the root word.

Synecdoche and metonymy in Shakespeare's works is often very confusing to a new student because he creates uses for words that they usually do not perform. This technique is often complicated and yet very subtle, which makes it difficult of a new student to dissect and understand. An example of these devices in one of Shakespeare's plays can be found in *The Merchant of Venice*. In warning his daughter, Jessica, to ignore the Christian revelries in the streets below, Shylock says:

Lock up my doors; and when you hear the drum
And the vile squealing of the wry-necked fife,
Clamber not you up to the casements then...
(I, v, ll. 30-32)

The phrase of importance in this quote is "the wry-necked fife." When a reader examines this phrase it does not seem to make sense; a fife is a cylinder-shaped instrument, there is no part of it that can be called a neck. The phrase then must be taken to refer to the fife-player, who has to twist his or her neck to play the fife. Fife, therefore, is a synecdoche for fife-player, much as boards is for stage. The trouble with understanding this phrase is that "vile squealing" logically refers to the sound of the fife, not the fife-player, and the reader might be led to take fife as the instrument because of the parallel reference to "drum" in the previous line. The best solution to this quandary is that Shakespeare uses the word fife to refer to both the instrument and the player. Both the player and the instrument are needed to complete the wordplay in this phrase, which, though difficult to understand to new readers, cannot be seen as a flaw since Shakespeare manages to convey two meanings with one word. This remarkable example of synecdoche illuminates Shakespeare's mastery of "verbal economy."

Shakespeare also uses vivid and imagistic wordplay through personification, in which human capacities and behaviors are attributed to inanimate objects. Bassanio, in *The Merchant of Venice*, almost speechless when Portia promises to marry him and share all her worldly wealth, states "my blood speaks to you in my veins…" (III, ii, l. 176). How deeply he must feel since even his blood can speak. Similarly, Portia, learning of the penalty that Antonio must pay for defaulting on his debt, tells Salerio, "There are some shrewd contents in yond same paper/That steals the color from Bassanio's cheek" (III, ii, ll. 243-244).

Another important facet of Shakespeare's rhetorical repertoire is his use of allusion. An allusion is a reference to another author or to an historical figure or event. Very often Shakespeare alludes to the heroes and heroines of Ovid's *Metamorphoses*. For example, in Cymbeline an entire room is decorated with images illustrating the stories from this classical work, and the heroine, Imogen, has been reading from this text. Similarly, in *Titus Andronicus* characters not only read directly from the *Metamorphoses*, but a subplot re-enacts one of the *Metamorphoses's* most famous stories, the rape and mutilation of Philomel.

Another way Shakespeare uses allusion is to drop names of mythological, historical and literary figures. In *The Taming of the*

Shrew, for instance, Petruchio compares Katharina, the woman whom he is courting, to Diana (II, i, l. 55), the virgin goddess, in order to suggest that Katharina is a man-hater. At times, Shakespeare will allude to well-known figures without so much as mentioning their names. In *Twelfth Night*, for example, though the Duke and Valentine are ostensibly interested in Olivia, a rich countess, Shakespeare asks his audience to compare the Duke's emotional turmoil to the plight of Acteon, whom the goddess Diana transforms into a deer to be hunted and killed by Acteon's own dogs:

Duke: That instant was I turn'd into a hart;
               And my desires, like fell and cruel hounds,
               E'er since pursue me.
               [...]
Valentine: But, like a cloistress, she will veiled walk
               And water once a day her chamber round....
               (I, i, page 2)

Shakespeare's use of puns spotlights his exceptional wit. His comedies in particular are loaded with puns, usually of a sexual nature. Puns work through the ambiguity that results when multiple senses of a word are evoked; homophones often cause this sort of ambiguity. In *Antony and Cleopatra*, Enobarbus believes "there is mettle in death" (I, ii, l. 146), meaning that there is "courage" in death; at the same time, mettle suggests the homophone metal, referring to swords made of metal causing death. In early editions of Shakespeare's work there was no distinction made between the two words. Antony puns on the word "earing," (I, ii, ll. 112-114) meaning both plowing (as in rooting out weeds) and hearing: he angrily sends away a messenger, not wishing to hear the message from his wife, Fulvia: "...O then we bring forth weeds,/when our quick minds lie still, and our ills told us/Is as our earing." If ill-natured news is planted in one's "hearing," it will render an "earing" (harvest) of ill-natured thoughts. A particularly clever pun, also in *Antony and Cleopatra*, stands out after Antony's troops have fought Octavius's men in Egypt: "We have beat him to his camp. Run one before,/And let the queen know of our gests" (IV, viii, ll. 1-2). Here "gests" means deeds (in this case, deeds of battle); it is also a pun on "guests," as though Octavius' slain soldiers were to be guests when buried in Egypt.

One should note that Elizabethan pronunciation was in several cases different from our own. Thus, modern readers, especially Americans, will miss out on the many puns based on homophones. The textual notes will point up many of these "lost" puns, however.

Shakespeare's sexual innuendoes can be either clever or tedious depending upon the speaker and situation. The modern reader should recall that sexuality in Shakespeare's time was far more complex than in ours and that characters may refer to such things as masturbation and homosexual activity. Textual notes in some editions will point out these puns but rarely explain them. An example of a sexual pun or innuendo can be found in *The Merchant of Venice* when Portia and Nerissa are discussing Portia's past suitors using innuendo to tell of their sexual prowess:

Portia: I pray thee, overname them, and as thou namest them, I will describe them, and according to my description level at my affection.

Nerrisa: First, there is the Neapolitan prince.

Portia: Ay, that's a colt indeed, for he doth nothing but talk of his horse, and he makes it a great appropriation to his own good parts that he can shoe him himself. I am much afeard my lady his mother played false with the smith.
           (I, ii, ll. 35-45)

The "Neapolitan prince" is given a grade of an inexperienced youth when Portia describes him as a "colt." The prince is thought to be inexperienced because he did nothing but "talk of his horse" (a pun for his penis) and his other great attributes. Portia goes on to say that the prince boasted that he could "shoe him [his horse] himself," a possible pun meaning that the prince was very proud that he could masturbate. Finally, Portia makes an attack upon the prince's mother, saying that "my lady his mother played false with the smith," a pun to say his mother must have committed adultery with a blacksmith to give birth to such a vulgar man having an obsession with "shoeing his horse."

It is worth mentioning that Shakespeare gives the reader hints when his characters might be using puns and innuendoes. In *The Merchant of Venice*, Portia's lines are given in prose when she is joking, or engaged in bawdy conversations. Later on the reader will notice that Portia's lines are rhymed in poetry, such as when she is talking in court or to Bassanio. This is Shakespeare's way of letting the reader know when Portia is jesting and when she is serious.

Shakespeare's Dramatic Verse

Finally, the reader will notice that some lines are actually rhymed verse while others are in verse without rhyme; and much of Shakespeare's drama is in prose. Shakespeare usually has his lovers speak in the language of love poetry which uses rhymed couplets. The archetypal example of this comes, of course, from *Romeo and Juliet*:

> The grey-ey'd morn smiles on the frowning night,
> Check'ring the eastern clouds with streaks of light,
> And fleckled darkness like a drunkard reels
> From forth day's path and Titan's fiery wheels.
> (II, iii, ll. 1-4)

Here it is ironic that Friar Lawrence should speak these lines since he is not the one in love. He, therefore, appears buffoonish and out of touch with reality. Shakespeare often has his characters speak in rhymed verse to let the reader know that the character is acting in jest, and vice-versa.

Perhaps the majority of Shakespeare's lines are in blank verse, a form of poetry which does not use rhyme (hence the name blank) but still employs a rhythm native to the English language, iambic pentameter, where every second syllable in a line of ten syllables receives stress. Consider the following verses from *Hamlet*, and note the accents and the lack of end-rhyme:

> The síngle ánd pecúliar lífe is bóund
> With áll the stréngth and ármor óf the mínd
> (III, iii, ll. 12-13)

The final syllable of these verses receives stress and is said to have a hard, or "strong," ending. A soft ending, also said to be "weak," receives no stress. In *The Tempest*, Shakespeare uses a soft ending to shape a verse that demonstrates through both sound (meter) and sense the capacity of the feminine to propagate:

> and thén I lóv'd thee
> And shów'd thee áll the quálitíes o' th' ísle,
> The frésh spríngs, bríne-pits, bárren pláce and fértile.
> (I, ii, ll. 338-40)

The first and third of these lines here have soft endings.

In general, Shakespeare saves blank verse for his characters of noble birth. Therefore, it is significant when his lofty characters speak in prose. Prose holds a special place in Shakespeare's dialogues; he uses it to represent the speech habits of the common people. Not only do lowly servants and common citizens speak in prose, but important, lower class figures also use this fun, at times ribald variety of speech. Though Shakespeare crafts some very ornate lines in verse, his prose can be equally daunting, for some of his characters may speechify and break into doubletalk in their attempts to show sophistication. A clever instance of this comes when the Third Citizen in *Coriolanus* refers to the people's paradoxical lack of power when they must elect Coriolanus as their new leader once Coriolanus has orated how he has courageously fought for them in battle:

> We have power in ourselves to do it, but
> it is a power that we have no power to do; for if he show
> us his wounds and tell us his deeds, we are to put our
> tongues into those wounds and speak for them; so, if he
> tell us his noble deeds, we must also tell him our noble
> acceptance of them. Ingratitude is monstrous, and for
> the multitude to be ingrateful were to make a monster
> of the multitude, of the which we, being members,
> should bring ourselves to be monstrous members.
> (II, ii, ll. 3-13)

Notice that this passage contains as many metaphors, hideous though they be, as any other passage in Shakespeare's dramatic verse.

When reading Shakespeare, paying attention to characters who suddenly break into rhymed verse, or who slip into prose after speaking in blank verse, will heighten your awareness of a character's mood and personal development. For instance, in *Antony and Cleopatra*, the famous military leader Marcus Antony usually speaks in blank verse, but also speaks in fits of prose (II, iii, ll. 43-46) once his masculinity and authority have been questioned. Similarly, in *Timon of Athens*, after the wealthy lord Timon abandons the city of Athens to live in a cave, he harangues anyone whom he encounters in prose (IV, iii, l. 331 ff.). In contrast, the reader should wonder why the bestial Caliban in *The Tempest* speaks in blank verse rather than in prose.

Implied Stage Action

When we read a Shakespearean play, we are reading a performance text. Actors interact through dialogue, but at the same time these actors cry, gesticulate, throw tantrums, pick up daggers, and compulsively wash murderous "blood" from their hands. Some of the action that takes place on stage is explicitly stated in stage directions. However, some of the stage activity is couched within the dialogue itself. Attentiveness to these cues is important as one conceives how to visualize the action. When Iago in *Othello* feigns concern for Cassio whom he himself has stabbed, he calls to the surrounding men, "Come, come:/Lend me a light" (V, i, ll. 86-87). It is almost sure that one of the actors involved will bring him a torch or lantern. In the same play, Emilia, Desdemona's maidservant, asks if she should fetch her lady's nightgown and Desdemona replies, "No, unpin me here" (IV, iii, l. 37). In Macbeth, after killing Duncan, Macbeth brings the murder weapon back with him. When he tells his wife that he cannot return to the scene and place the daggers to suggest that the king's guards murdered Duncan, she castigates him: "Infirm of purpose/Give me the daggers. The sleeping and the dead are but as pictures" (II, ii, ll. 50-52). As she exits, it is easy to visualize Lady Macbeth grabbing the daggers from her husband.

For 400 years, readers have found it greatly satisfying to work with all aspects of Shakespeare's language—the implied stage action, word choice, sentence structure, and wordplay—until all aspects come to life. Just as seeing a fine performance of a Shakespearean play is exciting, staging the play in one's own mind's eye, and revisiting lines to enrich the sense of the action, will enhance one's appreciation of Shakespeare's extraordinary literary and dramatic achievements.

Historical Background

Although fifteenth-century England had been a time of grave civil unrest and violence, by the time Shakespeare achieved prominence during Elizabeth and James' reigns it was enjoying a period of socio-political security and respect for the arts. Queen Elizabeth's reign extended from 1558 until 1603, when she was succeeded by the Scottish King James. Shakespeare received the patronage of both monarchs during his career as a playwright.

Elizabeth's reign was not without its tensions. There was an intense religious climate in which the Queen had to act decisively. The religious tensions that existed during Elizabeth's reign continued during James' reign, when he was pitted against the Puritans. England had gone to war with Spain. In other foreign affairs, the Queen was moderate, practicing a prudent diplomatic neutrality. There were, however, several plots on her life.

There was also evidence of progress. The nation experienced a commercial revolution. Elizabeth's government instituted two important social measures: "the Statute of Artificers" and the "Poor Laws," both of which were aimed at helping the people displaced and hurt by changing conditions. Laws were passed to regulate the economy. Explorers started to venture into the unknown for riches and land. The machinery of government was transformed. The administrative style of government replaced the household form of leadership.

The Elizabethan Age was an age that made a great writer like Shakespeare and his contemporaries possible. It produced excellent drama; Marlowe's *Tamburlaine* and Jonson's *Every Man in His Humour* are two examples. Sir Philip Sidney and Edmund

Spenser produced masterpieces during Elizabeth's reign. Shakespeare was in good company.

Shakespeare was well suited to the English Renaissance, with its new-found faith in the dignity and worth of the individual. Shakespeare profoundly understood human nature and provided us with some of the most imaginative character studies in drama. Shakespeare wrote for his company of players, known as the Lord Chamberlain's Men. He achieved considerable prosperity as a playwright. In addition to his artistic brilliance, Shakespeare wrote under the influence of the philosophy and effervescent spirit of the Elizabethan Age. Notably, we find the presence of the "Great Chain of Being," a view of life that started with Plato and Aristotle, in some of his plays. Furthermore, other ideas and social structures established in the Middle Ages still held sway during the early seventeenth century.

Shakespeare could display his universality and penetration in the public theater for his audience. His work, largely free of didactic and political motives, proved very entertaining.

The date of the composition of *Twelfth Night* is fixed around 1600. In using his creative powers on original sources, such as the Plautine *Gl'Ingannati* and Barnabe Rich's "Of Apolonius and Silla," Shakespeare was following a Renaissance tradition of working creatively with original situations. Shakespeare thus enjoyed artistic freedom and encouragement to produce a play like *Twelfth Night* for his audience, knowing that it would entertain viewers of all ages and status.

Master List of Characters

Orsino—*the Duke of Illyria, who is madly in love with Olivia.*

Olivia—*the countess with whom Orsino is in love and who rejects him.*

Curio—*one of the Duke's attendants.*

Valentine—*another gentlemen attending the Duke.*

Viola—*the female of a brother–sister pair of twins who enters Illyria disguised as Cesario and finds love.*

A Sea Captain—*a friend to Viola who comes ashore with her.*

Sir Toby Belch—*Olivia's uncle who drinks a lot and marries Maria.*

Maria—*Olivia's lady-in-waiting.*

Sir Andrew Aguecheek—*Sir Toby's friend who thinks he is a potential suitor for Olivia.*

Feste the Clown—*servant to Olivia who sings and provides entertainment.*

Malvolio—*steward to Olivia.*

Fabian—*another servant to Olivia.*

Antonio—*another sea captain who is friend to Viola and who comes ashore with Sebastian.*

Sebastian—*Viola's twin brother.*

First Officer—*officer in the service of the Duke.*

Second Officer—*also in the service of the Duke.*

A Priest—*marries Sebastian and Olivia.*

Musicians—*playing for Duke.*

Sailors—*come ashore with the Captain and Viola.*

Lords, Attendants

Summary of the Play

This is a play about love, placed in a festive atmosphere in which three couples are brought together happily. It opens with Orsino, the Duke of Illyria, expressing his deep love for the Countess Olivia. Meanwhile, the shipwrecked Viola disguises herself as a man and endeavors to enter the Duke's service. Although she has rejected his suit, the Duke then employs Viola, who takes the name of Cesario, to woo Olivia for him. Ironically, Cesario falls in love with the Duke, and Olivia falls in love with Cesario, who is really Viola disguised.

In the midst of this love triangle are the servants of Olivia's house and her Uncle Toby. The clown provides entertainment for the characters in both houses and speaks irreverently to them. He is the jester of the play. Maria, Olivia's woman, desires to seek revenge on Malvolio, Olivia's steward. To the delight of Sir Toby, Olivia's uncle, and his friend Sir Andrew, Maria comes up with a plot to drop love letters supposedly written by Olivia in Malvolio's path. When she does, they observe him, along with Fabian, another servant, as Malvolio falls for the bait. Believing that Olivia loves him, he makes a fool of himself.

The love plot moves along as Cesario goes to woo Olivia for the Duke. The second time that Cesario appears at Olivia's home Olivia openly declares her love for Cesario. All along, Sir Andrew has been nursing a hope to win Olivia's love. When he plans to give up on her, Sir Toby suggests that Sir Andrew fight with Cesario to impress Olivia. Cesario, however, refuses to fight.

In the meantime, Viola's brother, who is also shipwrecked, makes his way to safe lodging in Illyria with Antonio the sea captain. After the fight between Cesario and Sir Andrew begins, Antonio intervenes to save Cesario, whom he takes for Sebastian. But the Duke's officers promptly arrest Antonio for a past offense. Olivia later comes upon Sir Andrew and Sebastian wrangling at her house. Olivia, thinking Sebastian is Cesario, leads Sebastian to marriage in a nearby chapel.

The complications of identity are unraveled in the fifth act. Cesario finally reveals that he is Viola. Sebastian recognizes her as his sister. The Duke takes Viola up on her love offerings and proposes to her. Olivia assures Malvolio that she did not write the letter that so disturbed him. Sir Toby marries Maria in appreciation for her humiliating scheme.

Estimated Reading Time

You can read through *Twelfth Night* in about three and a half hours. But, when reading Shakespeare, you should plan to re-read at least one more time. When you read more carefully, paying attention to difficult words and Shakespeare's exquisite use of language, your reading time will necessarily increase. Your more careful reading may take about six hours.

SECTION TWO

Act I

Act I, Scene I (pages 1–2)

New Characters:

Orsino: *the Duke of Illyria, who is madly in love with Olivia*

Curio: *one of the Duke's attendants*

Valentine: *another gentleman attending the Duke*

Summary

The play opens at the Duke's palace in Illyria. The Duke is lovesick, and so the first 15 lines express his powerful love for the Countess Olivia. He pours forth sweet words of passion for his love object.

He desires to have music feed his appetite for love. He feels at first that he can't get enough of the energizing "food of love," but abruptly urges the musicians to stop playing: "Enough; no more."

Then, addressing the "spirit of love," he characterizes it as so broad a force that nothing can outdo or overcome it. Love is very, very powerful.

After this outpouring, one of the Duke's attendants, Curio, asks him if he plans to go hunting. But Orsino is in no mood for recreation; he is deeply in love. So his response is more than a mere "no." He says that his desire for Olivia has stronger control over him than anything else.

Valentine, another attendant, enters with words that the Duke does want to listen to because they concern Olivia. Valentine informs the Duke of Olivia's mourning. She is grieving the loss of her dead brother and plans to stay in mourning for a long time. So, for her, love is out!

This news frustrates the Duke. He realizes that he will not achieve the object of his desire—at least, not yet. He recognizes that Olivia is full of love, but is channeling it in another direction, away from him. Still, his lover's hope does not lessen as long as he feels that love will awaken in Olivia.

Analysis

The first scene leads us instantly into the major theme of the play—love. Shakespeare, the skillful dramatist, wastes no time in developing it. In so doing, he uses poetic devices such as metaphor, simile, puns, and synesthesia to reveal the extraordinary nature of true love.

The poetry of the Duke's opening speech clearly conveys the power of his love for Olivia:

> If music be the food of love, play on;
> Give me excess of it, that, surfeiting,
> The appetite may sicken, and so die.

The Duke uses a physical metaphor of eating food to show how strong his experience of love is. He commands the musicians to overwhelm him with music, so that his lingering appetite for Olivia will die. He is totally wrapped up in his love for her.

Further on in the Duke's opening speech, he directly addresses the "spirit of love," using a falconry metaphor to indicate the depth of true love. One doesn't have to be a hunter to appreciate the thought he tries to convey. Consider that the sky is such a broad and spacious area and that falcons can reach great heights while flying. The power of the poetry here rests in comparing the experience of love with the falcon reaching its highest point in flight. It's a dizzying image. The bird reaches its highest point and then must come down to lower heights. Just as the falcon cannot outdistance the sky, so "nought" can overdo or overwhelm the power of love. All other forces and influences will "fall into abatement" if they try to overwhelm love.

The Duke has ample time to walk around his palace being in love, doing nothing else. This sense of stasis suggests that the Duke is illustrating true love in its intensity as it lasts. He is engaged in the process of loving; he has not entered into a relationship with Olivia or any other woman as yet.

Accordingly, it might be said that the Duke is "in love with love." But his speeches in Scene I; while exalting the business of love, also demonstrate that he knows his love object to be Olivia, a real, breathing person, and he makes an effort to win her.

The title of the play, *Twelfth Night*, orients the reader toward another element in the play, namely, that of the playful and festive atmosphere of the action. The Twelfth Night of Christmas was an occasion for merriment when a "Lord of Misrule" was appointed to direct the festivities. It is interesting that Shakespeare associated this particular holiday with the theme of love. In the festival running through the play, love plays an important part as the characters meet and pair off. Plots and affairs of love are entertaining to be involved in. The meaning of the subtitle, "What You Will," is not so apparent to the reader. It is spoken by Olivia at the end of Act I to Malvolio when she instructs him to get rid of Cesario, who's come to woo her for the Duke. The casualness of the phrase reflects her loose attitude toward the Duke's love. It points up the contrast between her feelings and those of the Duke. Feste, the Clown, will later emphasize this mundane level of love. It may also suggest a satire on the foibles of man.

Study Questions

1. What is the major theme of the play?

2. With whom is the Duke in love?

3. In what kinds of poetry does the Duke express his love?

4. Is it entirely true that the Duke is "in love with love"?

5. What type of metaphor does the Duke use when he addresses the "spirit of love"?

6. What is the subtitle of the play?

7. Toward what does the title *Twelfth Night* orient the reader?

8. What recreation does Curio ask the Duke about?

9. What is "Twelfth Night"?

10. What kind of part does love play in the festival atmosphere of the play?

Answers

1. Love is the major theme of the play.

2. The Duke is in love with Olivia.

3. The Duke's poetry contains metaphors, puns, synesthesia, and similes.

4. No, it is not completely true because the Duke is clearly in love with Olivia, a specific person.

5. He uses a metaphor drawn from falconry when he addresses the "spirit of love."

6. The subtitle of the play is "What You Will."

7. The title orients the reader toward the playful and festive atmosphere of the action.

8. Curio asks the Duke if he is going hunting.

9. "Twelfth Night" is a holiday and occasion for merriment.

10. Love plays an important part as the characters meet and pair off.

Suggested Essay Topics

1. Does the Duke's opening speech show praise for Olivia in particular or for the experience of love in general? Explain your answer by citing specific lines.

2. What kind of judgment would you make about the Duke's character based on his speech and behavior in the first scene? Discuss why you get this impression. Discuss either several specific qualities or one generalized personality trait.

Act I, Scene II (pages 2–4)

New Characters:

Viola: *the female of a twin brother–sister pair, who enters Illyria disguised as Cesario and finds love*

A Sea Captain: *a friend to Viola who comes ashore with her*

Summary

The setting of this scene is appropriately away from the majestic atmosphere of the Duke's palace. We meet Viola and a captain on a seacoast. Viola's practical nature serves to complement the Duke's romantic character.

Shipwrecked, Viola asks the Captain and sailors where she is. The Captain tells her that they are in a region called "Illyria." Her brother, who had also been on the ship with her, is separated from them, which causes Viola to wonder if he has drowned. The Captain suggests that he may still be alive because he last saw him struggling to stay afloat.

The Captain was born and raised in Illyria, and he knows about the Duke's courtship with Olivia. The Captain relates Olivia's disinclination to accept Orsino's pledge, as he has heard from gossip.

Upon hearing this, Viola is moved to serve Olivia. But the Captain tells her that that is impossible. Olivia has closed herself off to any new relationships while she deeply mourns the loss of her brother.

Viola quickly gets another idea. She decides to serve the Duke instead, as his eunuch. Since she is a woman, that plan will require a disguise: "Conceal me what I am." This plan is very practical, for it utilizes a disguise. Viola claims to have a purpose in assuming a disguise, but, at this point, it is not clear exactly what she wants to achieve. She even says, "What else may hap to time I will commit."

Analysis

This scene shifts the thematic emphasis to a practical, commonsense aspect of love. In so doing, Shakespeare is implying that there's more to love than mere poetry. It's all right to put one's loved one up on a pedestal, but it also becomes necessary to find a way to get her down and together with the wooer. Valentine, the Duke's servant, had only gone to Olivia to report the Duke's love for her and obtain a favorable reply. Viola represents a viable plan of action to bring the two together in love. Her offerings of money to the Captain, for example, symbolize this practical side to her character. Money is a tool and a means to an end. Viola is well aware that money represents a way to get people to do what she wants.

The disguise plan has been used a lot in Shakespeare's plays. Here, as in *Measure for Measure* and *As You Like It*, a noble character puts on a mask in order to influence the behavior of other characters. Since Viola desires to serve the Duke, her goal may be to help make the love match a reality for him.

Relevant to her noble motivation is Viola's stating of a significant Shakespearean theme, that is, appearances versus the reality underlying them. Shakespeare knew all too well that appearances can be deceiving. People seem other than what they are in order to deceive or hurt other people. Viola comments perceptively on the Captain's true character. He is authentic and can be trusted. Her valuing of an authentic character implies that her own motivation is for the Duke's benefit.

Viola repeats the music image of the first scene. True to her character as we've seen it thus far, she has in mind a specific practical use for music. She plans to "speak to him in many sorts of music." Clearly, Viola wants to get on the Duke's good side and help him. So, she will use music to do so. Notice the active/passive contrast of each character's use of music. Whereas the Duke passively requests that his musicians play music so it will fill him to overflow, Viola contemplates the active use of music to get into the good graces of the Duke.

Study Questions

1. Where do we first meet Viola?
2. What happened to Viola's brother?
3. What kind of nature does Viola have?

4. What does Shakespeare imply about love in his shift of thematic emphasis?

5. What device does Viola use to get into the Duke's service?

6. Is it clear what Viola wants to achieve in the Duke's service?

7. How does Shakespeare symbolize Viola's practical side?

8. Is *Twelfth Night* the only play that involves a character putting on a disguise?

9. What other significant Shakespearean theme does Viola state?

10. What image that the Duke employs does Viola also use?

Answers

1. We first meet Viola on a seacoast.

2. He was separated from Viola when the ship sank.

3. Viola has a practical nature.

4. Shakespeare implies that there's more to love than mere poetry.

5. Viola uses the disguise device to get into the Duke's service.

6. No, it is not clear as yet what Viola's specific goal is.

7. Shakespeare symbolizes Viola's practical side by having her offer money in payment for favors to her.

8. No, Shakespeare has used disguised characters in other plays.

9. Viola states the theme of "appearances versus reality."

10. Viola repeats the music image of the first scene.

Suggested Essay Topics

1. Viola comments on the deceptiveness of appearances. People aren't always what they seem to be. Why do you think this theme would be significant in a play that deals with love? Cite evidence from the play to support your answer.

2. Why does the love object have to come down from the altar of the lover's worship? Why, that is, can't the Duke keep praising Olivia forever? How does Viola make it clear that there's more to being in love than just poetry? Make sure you present your topic sentences clearly in the essay.

Act I, Scene III (pages 4–7)

New Characters:

Sir Toby Belch: *Olivia's uncle, who drinks a lot*

Maria: *Olivia's lady-in-waiting*

Sir Andrew Aguecheek: *Sir Toby's friend, who thinks he is a potential suitor for Olivia*

Summary

This scene is set in Olivia's house, but we do not as yet meet Olivia. She is in extended mourning. Sir Toby, her uncle, opens with a question about Olivia. He is talking to Maria, Olivia's lady-in-waiting, who responds with a complaint about Toby's late carousing.

Maria refers to Sir Toby's friend, Sir Andrew, as a fool. She heard that Sir Toby had brought him to the house to woo Olivia. Sir Toby, on the other hand, praises the many virtues his friend possesses. He is handsome, has a good income, and speaks several languages. Furthermore, they are drinking buddies.

When Sir Andrew enters, Sir Toby immediately urges him on Maria, "board her, woo her, assail her," though Sir Andrew misunderstands him at first. As Sir Toby's meaning dawns on him, he asserts that he wouldn't do such a thing in Olivia's house.

Before departing, Maria invites Sir Andrew for a drink. Sir Toby realizes that her invitation was made in a joking manner, and he engages Sir Andrew in a playful conversation. Sir Andrew talks of leaving, having lost hope of winning Olivia's love. He believes the Count Orsino has a much better chance for her than he does. Nonetheless, Sir Toby reassures him that his chances are still good because Orsino is not the kind of man Olivia is looking for. This reassurance encourages Sir Andrew to stay a month longer.

So, continuing their conversation together, Sir Toby questions his friend's dancing ability. Sir Andrew says that he's quite a capable dancer. They then plan to go partying together.

Analysis

The characters of Maria and Sir Toby put us in touch with a lower class of people in Illyria; that is, they do not belong to the aristocracy as do Orsino and Olivia. This is a play for all kinds of people; love is for everyone. The disguise trick suggests this notion. It doesn't matter what your financial or social status is in love because true love does not play favorites. That is why Sir Andrew and Malvolio can entertain hopes of winning Olivia's love. Love is an experience that occurs between two human beings. A disguise can prove this statement because if you can conceal who or what you truly are, then it follows that it doesn't matter what your real identity is. Love can blossom. All is fair in love.

A note of competition enters the play in this scene. Sir Toby believes Sir Andrew to be a proper suitor for his niece. Despite his praise, however, the scene leaves us with the impression that Sir Andrew may not be so appropriate. Maria, for one, knocks him. By suggesting Sir Andrew for Olivia—in the light of his iffy status—Shakespeare asserts the universality of his love theme.

Beyond that, these characters illustrate the party-and-fun atmosphere, as implied in the title's holiday. They drink, dance, and flirt with the ladies, everything one would expect at a wild, exciting festival. There's a lighthearted playfulness all through the play; Sir Toby and Andrew seem to keep the celebration going. Their roles may be to suggest that liveliness and fun should surround the process of falling in love.

Notice how Shakespeare uses the language to reveal Sir Toby's free spirit. He parodies Maria's use of the word "exception." His repetition of the word "confine" with a new meaning is an instance of the figurative device called "ploce." Maria uses it in the sense of "keep," while Sir Toby switches to the sense of "dress." There's a sly defiance in this switch of senses that reflects his high-spirited nature. This example of "ploce" and others in this scene lend a sharp emphasis to the dialogue.

The scene ends with Sir Toby introducing a succession of "dance" images. This imagery both characterizes Sir Toby as the representative of partying that he is, and it strengthens the overall presence of a festival in Illyria.

Study Questions

1. Do we meet Olivia in this scene?

2. What is Sir Andrew's relationship to Sir Toby?

3. What did Maria hear about Sir Andrew's purpose for being in the house?

4. What does the presence of Maria and Sir Toby as characters imply?

5. Who brings in a note of competition to the scene?

6. Does Sir Andrew seem an appropriate suitor for Olivia?

7. What else do Sir Toby and Sir Andrew illustrate in the play?

8. How does Shakespeare reveal Sir Toby's free spirit?

9. What is "ploce"?

10. What type of imagery does Sir Toby introduce at the end of the scene?

Answers

1. No, we do not meet Olivia in this scene.

2. They are friends.

3. Maria heard that Sir Toby brought him to the house to woo Olivia.

4. They imply that love is for all kinds of people, no matter what their status is.

5. Sir Andrew brings in a note of competition.

6. No, the scene leaves us with the impression that Sir Andrew may not be an appropriate suitor for Olivia.

7. Sir Toby and Sir Andrew illustrate the party-and-fun atmosphere, as implied in the title's holiday.

8. Shakespeare reveals Sir Toby's free spirit through the language.

9. "Ploce" is the repetition of a word in a different sense.

10. Sir Toby introduces a succession of "dance" images.

Suggested Essay Topics

1. Sir Andrew may not be a good suitor for Olivia. Defend this thesis statement referring to specific examples from the dialogue.

2. Analyze the dance imagery found on page 7. Why do you think Shakespeare included it in the dialogue? With what aspect of the play does it tie in? What does it emphasize?

Act I, Scene IV (pages 8–9)

Summary

We find Viola (now named "Cesario") on her fourth day in the Duke's palace, her disguise having gained her the access she wished. Valentine is amazed, in fact, at how much favor she has already gained with the Duke.

The Duke assigns Cesario the task of pursuing Olivia for him. He urges him to be aggressive: "Be clamorous and leap all civil bounds." The Duke is confident that Cesario can effectively persuade Olivia to respond to his true passion. Cesario is doubtful.

Part of the Duke's confidence owes to his intuition of Cesario's real feminine qualities. He implies, in other words, that she can play the womanly matchmaker role well. He promises him a reward if he is successful in his undertaking.

Viola's last lines allude to another plot strand in the play, her love for the Duke, which she cannot reveal because of her disguise.

Analysis

It is appropriate to consider a definition of the type of play (or "genre") that Twelfth Night is. *Twelfth Night* belongs to a species of drama known as "comedy." We expect the course of action in a comedy to be different from that in a tragedy. As M.H. Abrams puts it in *A Glossary of Literary Terms*:

> Romantic comedy, as developed by Shakespeare and some of his Elizabethan contemporaries, is concerned with a love affair that involves a beautiful and idealized heroine (sometimes disguised as a man); the course of this love does not run smooth, but overcomes all difficulties to end in a happy union.

Twelfth Night contains both of these elements and a lot more. The definition enlightens us about the ending; it will be a happy one. In comedy, love conquers all. Northrop Frye makes it clear that comedy is "community-oriented, its vision has a social significance. This vision calls for the establishing of society as we would like it." (Frye, 286)

Recall, therefore, that up until the fourth scene, the Duke's love is virtually the "talk of the town." Not only does the Duke brim with lyrical expression of his love, but the other characters are also aware of his infatuation. This tight interweaving of the Orsino courtship strand develops the love theme quite nicely.

This scene offers an inkling as to a slight alteration in the Duke's impassioned stance toward Olivia. Cesario's brief stay has exerted a subtle influence on him. Orsino closes the scene with a display of common sense that moves him momentarily away from the love-filled garden he's been in. He judges Cesario's ability to perform the errand and offers him wealth if he succeeds.

Study Questions

1. What is Viola's male name?

2. What task does the Duke assign Cesario?

3. For whom does Cesario feel love for?

4. To what genre does the play *Twelfth Night* belong?

5. What kind of an ending do we expect in comedy?

6. What kind of vision does comedy have, according to Northrop Frye?

7. What is the community of Illyria doing about the Duke's love?

8. How does the Duke respond to Cesario's doubts that Olivia is too "abandon'd to her sorrow" to listen to his suit?

9. Does the Duke change?

10. What does Orsino display at the end of the scene?

Answers

1. Viola's male name is "Cesario."

2. The Duke assigns Cesario the task of pursuing Olivia for him.

3. Cesario feels love for the Duke.

4. *Twelfth Night* belongs to the genre of "comedy."

5. We expect a happy ending in comedy.

6. Comedy's vision has a social significance.

7. The community in Illyria is well aware of and talking about the Duke's love.

8. The Duke tells him to "be clamorous and leap all civil bounds."

9. The Duke's impassioned stance toward Olivia changes slightly.

10. Orsino displays common sense at the end of the scene.

Suggested Essay Topics

1. Think of your efforts to win a sweetheart when you've fallen in love, or what you might do to win one. In what ways would those efforts be similar or different from Cesario's endeavors to woo Olivia for the Duke?

2. Consider once again the definition of "Romantic comedy" stated earlier. Why do you think the society of a given era would desire a happy ending? Would you like to see *Twelfth Night* end in another way than it does?

Act I, Scene V (pages 9–17)

New Characters:

Olivia: *the countess with whom Orsino is in love and who rejects him*

Clown: *servant to Olivia who sings and provides entertainment*

Malvolio: *steward to Olivia*

Summary

This scene opens with Maria and the Clown engaged in conversation. Maria, wondering where the Clown has been, tells him that he'll be punished for his absence unless he has good reason for it. This threat fails to scare the Clown, as he shows in his offhand replies.

The Clown is equally offhand with Olivia when she enters. He responds to her with insult, ironically calling her a "fool." Although she tries to get rid of him, the Clown prevails on her to prove that she is the fool. To that end, he questions her about her mourning her brother's death.

Unoffended, Olivia turns to her steward Malvolio for his opinion of the Clown. An exchange of insults follows her question. The Clown puts down Malvolio and Malvolio puts down the Clown. Malvolio considers the Clown a stupid, useless character. Olivia sides with the Clown, even calling Malvolio an egotist, because the Clown is only playing his role as fool properly.

Maria announces Cesario's arrival. Olivia is not in the mood to listen to a suit from the Duke. Malvolio returns to Olivia to tell her that Cesario stubbornly refuses to leave until Olivia will speak with him. Olivia wonders what kind of man he is. She allows him to enter and puts on a veil.

Cesario begins by showering lover's compliments on Olivia. Cesario makes a point of the fact that her suit is memorized. Everything he will say has been rehearsed beforehand.

Shortly after starting his speech of love, Cesario requests to see Olivia's face. Olivia complies and is met with praise for her "beauty truly blent." Cesario further affirms the Duke's passion for Olivia, expressing a hope that Olivia will reciprocate the Duke's love.

Unfortunately for the Duke, Olivia has no desire to love him. Cesario does not quite believe her rejection of Orsino. He can do little more than express a hope that Olivia will return the Duke's love, before he exits.

Olivia then reveals that she has been taken with the youth. His charms have worked their subtle ways on Olivia's eyes. So, she sends Malvolio after him with a token of her newfound affection, a ring. Her final words intimate some confusion about what is happening to her.

Analysis

The original love connection of the Duke admiring Olivia has gone awry by the end of this scene. We witness two twists: Viola states her attraction to Orsino, and Olivia reveals a liking for Cesario. These two twists suggest that, for Shakespeare, love is truly a subjective experience. When a person sees a potential sweetheart and falls in love, he or she feels it in his or her own heart and mind. One cannot be forced to love another by the sheer strength of the other's attraction, as the Duke's suit might imply.

Another way that Shakespeare emphasizes the subjective nature of love is through the Clown's speech. The Clown stands in counterpoint to the Duke in respect to his attitude toward Olivia. The smitten Duke utters his passionate feeling for Olivia, but the Clown's insults are couched in a jarringly logical manner. The former exalts Olivia; the latter belittles her. The Clown insists on proving Olivia a "fool." This slighting of Olivia reveals her to be a real person rather than the idealized goddess that the Duke opens the play with.

Shakespeare's plays have fools and clowns in them, whose speech very often has relevance to the action. The most famous example is Lear's fool, who utters profound commentary on Lear's plight. The Clown's role in Twelfth Night is a bit more subtle. As noted, the Clown's self-conscious reference to words and logic provide an indirect commentary on the Duke's love.

In an obvious way, the Clown is the clown of the party in the play. His wordplay and attitude toward Olivia demonstrate that he's enjoying the amusement that is found in a festive atmosphere. In keeping with the fun-filled atmosphere, Sir Toby makes a drunken entrance to comment briefly on Cesario's arrival.

Cesario's prepared speech for Olivia, on Orsino's behalf, contains an extended theological metaphor, which Olivia picks up on and carries forward. Cesario contends that he has a sacred message for Olivia. The loftiness of the theological metaphor reflects the great value placed on Orsino's suit. His love is sacred; Olivia is his goddess. A special bond is thus formed between Cesario and Olivia in view of the way Olivia responds to the theological language of his speech. Perhaps she is valuing the speaker more than the speech.

Cesario finishes his effort to persuade Olivia with speech that has not been studied. He includes hyperbole to emphasize the Duke's passion (page 16). Cesario earnestly believes that Olivia should return the Duke's offer of love. He regards her closed-mindedness as cruel.

Study Questions

1. What does Maria threaten the Clown with?

2. What kind of attitude does the Clown evidence toward Olivia?

3. What does the Clown try to prove about Olivia?

4. What is the name of Olivia's steward?

5. What does Olivia put on before speaking with Cesario?

6. Who falls in love with whom in this scene?

7. What do the two love twists we've witnessed suggest?

8. Which character serves to emphasize the subjective nature of "love" ?

9. In what manner are the Clown's insults couched?

10. What type of metaphor does Cesario use to lend emphasis to the great love the Duke holds for Olivia?

Answers

1. Maria threatens the Clown with punishment for his absence.

2. The Clown evidences an offhand attitude toward Olivia.

3. The Clown tries to prove that Olivia is a fool.

4. Malvolio is Olivia's steward.

5. Olivia puts on a veil before speaking with Cesario.

6. Olivia falls in love with Cesario.

7. The love twists suggest just how subjective is the experience of love.

8. The Clown's speech emphasizes the subjective nature of "love."

9. The Clown's insults are couched in a jarringly logical manner.

10. Cesario uses an extended theological metaphor to reflect the Duke's great love.

Suggested Essay Topics

1. How does the Clown prove that Olivia is a fool? Is he correct or incorrect in his assessment? Explain your answer with evidence found in the text.

2. How many love strands does the first act contain? Who is involved in them? Where do the relationships stand by the end of Act I in relation to how they will eventually develop?

SECTION THREE

Act II

Act II, Scene I (pages 18–19)

New Characters:

Antonio: *a sea captain, friend to Sebastian, who wishes to serve him*

Sebastian: *Viola's twin brother, who survives the shipwreck and initially believes Viola has drowned*

Summary

This short scene serves the purpose of letting us know that Sebastian, Viola's twin brother, has reached the shores of Illyria. We need this information to prepare our understanding of later scenes.

Sebastian tells us a little about himself, thus informing us that he has a twin sister. He thinks that she drowned while he managed to gain safety.

He wishes to separate from Antonio and wander about the area. But shortly afterward, he contradicts himself in this intention by stating that he, specifically, wants to go to "the Count Orsino's court." Although Antonio offers to serve Sebastian, he cannot go immediately with him to Orsino's court because he has "many enemies" there. Yet, we will learn that Antonio's affection for Sebastian is strong enough to prompt him to follow after him eventually.

ACT II, SCENE I

Analysis

Notice the very straightforward and formal manner in which these men talk to one another. Since this scene serves an informative purpose, the formal dialogue is most appropriate. There is very little poetry in this scene. They are not expressing their love for a woman as Orsino was doing in the first scene. The dialogue serves up numerous indications that its purpose here is just to inform. Antonio starts the dialogue with a straightforward yes-or-no question: "Will you stay no longer?" Sebastian gives his answer. Then Antonio makes a request whose very words explicitly suggest that this scene is providing the audience with information: "Let me know of you whither you are bound." Finally, Sebastian states background information in his next speech.

The contrast between the formal prose of this scene and the poetry of the love speeches should teach us about Shakespeare's use of language. Poetry expresses feeling, often strong feeling, so using it to reveal the depth of one's love is a fine touch. Prose aims to inform and enlighten us about a particular subject or issue, and it is often, though not always, free of the embellishments and imagination of poetry.

The use of shipwrecked twins in a romantic plot, such as in *Twelfth Night*, is not an idea original to Shakespeare. As with most of his plays, he used source materials to inspire him with characters and plots. L.G. Salingar enlightens us as to the way in which Shakespeare manipulated his sources:

> There are four essential characters to Gl'Ingannati [a Sienese comedy], Bandello [story], Riche [story], and Shakespeare; namely, a lover, a heroine in his service disguised as a page, her twin brother (who at first has disappeared), and a second heroine. The basic elements common to all four plots are: the heroine's secret love for her master; her employment as go-between, leading to the complication of a cross-wooing; and a final solution by means of the unforeseen arrival of the missing twin.

Even Shakespeare's mastery required original source materials on which to work.

Study Questions

1. What is Antonio's occupation?

2. What relation does Sebastian hold to Viola?

3. What does Sebastian think has happened to Viola?

4. Where do Antonio and Sebastian find themselves in this scene?

5. What purpose does this scene serve?

6. How would you characterize the style of the dialogue?

7. Where does Sebastian say he is headed?

8. What does Antonio want to do for Sebastian?

9. Name one source for *Twelfth Night*.

10. Essentially, what do the sources and the play *Twelfth Night* have in common?

Answers

1. Antonio is a sea captain.

2. Sebastian is Viola's brother.

3. Sebastian thinks that Viola has drowned.

4. They find themselves on Illyria's shore.

5. The purpose of this scene is to inform us about Viola's twin brother.

6. The style is one of formal, straightforward prose.

7. Sebastian says he is headed for Orsino's court.

8. Antonio wishes to serve Sebastian.

9. The sources for *Twelfth Night* are Gl'Ingannati, Bandello, and Riche.

10. The sources have the four essential characters and the plot in common with Shakespeare.

Suggested Essay Topics

1. Name one characteristic of poetic language and one of prose. After you state those, select one speech in the play that contains poetry and another from Act II, Scene I that contains prose, and explain the differences you notice between the two. Allow your imagination to explore the significance of the two different styles.

2. An important issue to be aware of when discussing characters' motivations and fates is that of "free will" versus "determinism or fate." Define these two concepts. And then consider Sebastian's first speech, in the light of that issue. Does Sebastian feel that he is in full control of things?

Act II, Scene II (pages 19–20)

Summary

Malvolio catches up with Cesario to give him the ring from Olivia. Naturally, he is surprised inasmuch as he knows he did not leave a ring. Malvolio also repeats Olivia's desire not to have any further dealings with Orsino. Before leaving, Malvolio puts the ring on the ground.

Left alone on stage, Cesario utters a soliloquy in which he expresses his confusion over the ring. He now realizes that Olivia has fallen in love with him. "She loves me, sure," he asserts. He acknowledges that the disguise must be responsible for stirring up her love. He finishes up the soliloquy wondering how this mistaken love on his part and frustrated love on his master's part will be resolved. As matters currently stand, there is a mess for all the lovers involved. Time will bring in the solutions.

Analysis

It is useful to understand the function of a soliloquy in drama. Sometimes a playwright cannot include important information about character or plot in the dialogue, so a soliloquy may become necessary.

> Soliloquy is the act of talking to oneself, silently or aloud. In drama it denotes the convention by which a character, alone on the stage, utters his thoughts aloud; the playwright uses this device as a convenient way to convey directly to the audience information about a character's motives, intentions, and state of mind, as well as for purposes of general exposition. (Abrams, 180)

In this scene, Cesario certainly makes an important commentary about the love situation while alone on stage. A soliloquy like the one he utters is true to the character of Cesario we've seen so far.

His words continue to reflect his role as representative of the practical, commonsense aspect of love in this play. He very logically takes account of Olivia and Orsino's feelings. True, he may be capable of such intense feelings for another person, but he realizes that people have to get along in the real world each day, too. This play gives us the feeling that the depiction of love would somehow be incomplete if it emphasized just the romance and passion of Orsino and Olivia's feelings. Love can still see the beloved as an ordinary human being.

Critics have argued over how to interpret Malvolio. The issue relates to Malvolio's character and the significance of the comic plot centered on him. Consider how dutiful and nonchalant he appears in this scene. He brings the ring, delivers Olivia's message, and takes off. We can start to form our opinion of his character.

In his soliloquy, Cesario repeats the motif of "appearances versus reality." Every instance of a motif should enhance our understanding of the playwright's views on that particular subject.

> Disguise, I see, thou art a wickedness,
> Wherein the pregnant enemy does much.
> How easy is it for the proper-false
> In women's waxen hearts to set their forms!

These lines express his concern that appearances are deceiving. In this context, Olivia has fallen in love with Cesario's outer masculinity, which causes him to realize that a mask can lead someone into love, regardless of the true character of the person beneath it. It is not Cesario's intention, however, to seduce Olivia.

Study Questions

1. Why does Malvolio seek Cesario?
2. Whose ring is it?
3. What kind of speech is it that Cesario utters?
4. What does Malvolio emphasize to Cesario?
5. Where does Malvolio put the ring?
6. What does Cesario feel about the ring?
7. Who has fallen in love with Cesario?
8. What does Cesario wonder in the latter part of the soliloquy?
9. What motif does Cesario repeat in his soliloquy?
10. What is the critics' attitude toward Malvolio?

Answers

1. Malvolio seeks Cesario to give him a ring.
2. It is a ring from Olivia.
3. Cesario utters a soliloquy.
4. Malvolio emphasizes that Olivia wants Orsino to stop his wooing.
5. Malvolio places the ring on the ground.
6. Cesario feels confused about the ring.
7. Olivia has fallen in love with Cesario.
8. Cesario wonders how the mistaken love will be resolved.
9. Cesario repeats the motif of "appearances versus reality."
10. Critics have argued over how to interpret Malvolio.

Suggested Essay Topics

1. Does Cesario's soliloquy add to our knowledge of character or plot? Read it carefully and explain your answer. Be sure to specify whose character and which plot.

2. Look carefully at the couplet closing Cesario's soliloquy: "O time! thou must untangle this, not I;/It is too hard a knot for me to untie!" To what knot is he referring? How does this knot eventually become unravelled in the play? How is this resolution instructive in respect to the theme of love?

Act II, Scene III (pages 20–25)

Summary

In case we'd forgotten about the merriment of the play, this scene puts us back in Olivia's house and opens with the leader of the party, Sir Toby. If we follow the love plot of the previous scene, we are then led astray by what these two men say. They begin by talking about going to bed early. Sir Toby says that going to bed after midnight is equal to going to bed early. Toby calls for some wine to have with their food.

When Feste the Clown enters, Andrew compliments his singing voice and his skill displayed in entertainment the previous night: "Why, this is best fooling, when all is done." Then, continuing in this vein, Sir Toby calls for another frequently used element in Shakespeare's plays—a song. Feste suggests either a love song or a song with a moral. Naturally, a love song is apropos. The Clown sings a song that recalls the Duke's elevated emotion of the first scene; he also defines "love." Very pleased with the Clown's song, they engage him in some more singing.

Nevertheless, Maria enters and chides them for their nonsense. Sir Toby banters with her, as is appropriate to his role as "lord of misrule," (to use the holiday expression). Malvolio's questions refer to their purpose as the merrymakers in the play. His question, "Do ye make an ale-house of my lady's house?", best points up the intersection of the holiday atmosphere and the love theme, which constitutes the play's peculiar blend. Malvolio seriously restates his lady's displeasure with Sir Toby's revels. What follows, to Malvolio's chagrin, is more singing and wine-drinking. Malvolio departs with an insult from Maria.

It is at this point that the comic plot is hatched. Maria reveals that she wants revenge on Malvolio, and Sir Toby and Andrew go right along with her scheme. Maria believes that she is wreaking revenge on Malvolio's Puritan character. Maria explains the plot: it involves dropping letters in Malvolio's way, supposedly written by Olivia (in her own hand), which will lead him to believe that Olivia is professing her love to him. They are to delight in the spectacle.

Analysis

This scene is a good illustration of what L.G. Salingar (quoting Enid Welsford) characterizes as Shakepeare's transmuting "into poetry the quintessence of the Saturnalia." There is plenty of wine and singing running through a scene that also gives us the springboard for Malvolio's pending humiliation. To clarify this important element of the play, Salingar further adds, "The sub-plot shows a prolonged season of misrule, or 'uncivil rule,' in Olivia's household, with Sir Toby turning night into day; there are drinking, dancing, and singing, . . . and the gulling of an unpopular member of the household." So, by this point, the significance of the title should be quite clear.

It is noteworthy how appropriate the song from Feste the Clown is, for it defines love. This is a play that illustrates the theme of love, showing a particular vision of the love experience. The song is divided into two halves: the first half resembles the outpourings that we've already read from the Duke. It expresses praise and longing for the love object. The second half embodies the theme, "What is love?" The definition emphasizes the intensity of feeling such as the Duke has shown. Thus it has little relevance to Cesario's role in the play. There is a double-faceted nature to love. (Some may even see or feel more facets.) Willard Gaylin puts it this way in his *Rediscovering Love*:

> Obviously loving and being loved can and should coexist in one relationship—there is no real conflict between

the two. One may so dominate the psychological needs of an individual as to exclude the other [as we clearly see with Orsino], but they have a natural compatibility. (Gaylin, 108)

In the opening scene, the Duke has no relationship with Olivia as he utters his love. Cesario enters his service to engender a loving relationship for him.

As for the controversy surrounding Malvolio, there is no reason to expect that he take part in the revelling. So, Maria's criticism of his being too straitlaced doesn't hold a lot of water. He performs his service earnestly and dutifully for his lady. We ought to ponder whether revenge is a fitting motive for the deception to follow. Some readers might conclude that Maria and Sir Toby resent Malvolio because he appears moralistic and judgmental.

Study Questions

1. What does going to bed after midnight mean for Sir Toby?

2. What does Sir Andrew call Feste the Clown?

3. What ability of the Clown does Sir Andrew compliment?

4. What do Sir Toby and Andrew offer to Feste for his singing?

5. What two types of songs does the Clown suggest?

6. What does the Clown's song define?

7. In keeping with the holiday tradition, what title can we apply to Sir Toby?

8. What plot is hatched in this scene?

9. What is Maria's motive for the scheme?

10. What does Maria plan to drop in Malvolio's way?

Answers

1. For Sir Toby, going to bed after midnight means going to bed early.

2. Sir Andrew calls Feste "the fool."

3. Sir Andrew compliments the Clown's singing voice.

4. They offer him money.

5. The Clown suggests either a love song or a song with a moral.

6. The Clown's song defines "love."

7. Sir Toby can take on the title of the "lord of misrule."

8. The comic plot is hatched in this scene.

9. Maria's motive for the scheme is revenge.

10. Maria plans to drop letters in Malvolio's way.

Suggested Essay Topics

1. Describe the fun and festive atmosphere that makes up most of this scene. What role does Feste the Clown play in it? Cite specific lines to strengthen your description. Do you enjoy the playfulness? Why or why not?

2. Analyze Maria's speeches in this scene. Explain carefully her motive to entrap Malvolio. Do you believe that she is justified in doing it?

Act II, Scene IV (pages 25–29)

Summary

In this scene, we are back at the Duke's palace. Once again, the Duke wants to hear some music, the food for his love. He calls for the Clown, who happens not to be there at the moment. While waiting for the Clown to be located, he speaks with Cesario.

The Duke affirms his true love. He continues to be the passionate lover who yearns for his beloved. His emotions, as a lover, are topsy-turvy.

The Duke surmises that Cesario had once also been in love, as he currently is. He answers "yes" that she was of the same age and temperament as the Duke. He responds with his belief that the woman should be the younger of the pair, so as to ensure that the love remain robust.

The Clown returns and Orsino is eager for a love song, a song that deals with the innocence of love, such as he is experiencing. The emphasis in the Clown's song is prophetic. It focuses on the Duke's frustration with and failure to obtain Olivia, his heart's desire. The lover in the song is "slain by a fair cruel maid." In short, it's a song of unrequited love.

Interestingly, in spite of the Duke's praise for this song, the Clown insults Orsino in a manner similar to the way he insulted Olivia in Act I. The Clown suggests that he lacks consistency and direction, though the logical form of his expression is not so apparent as in his insult to Olivia.

The Duke sends Cesario to Olivia to woo her for him. Cesario warns him that Olivia is not open to romance with him. Cesario asks the Duke if he would love a woman just because she had an intense attraction to him. The Duke does not think that that is a valid comparison, suggesting that a man's love is more powerful. Cesario disagrees with the Duke's proposition. Women are capable of very strong love attachments. Cesario, in fact, refers to his father's daughter as an example.

Analysis

The Duke wants to hear some music. This is the same request he makes at the start of Act I. This suggests that his love is still strong. The frustration has failed to extinguish the fire in his heart. Again, he is in the passive role of wanting the music to work on his feelings. His request for Feste to sing again should also remind us of the festive spirit.

As the Duke speaks to Cesario, we find him in the same infatuated frame of mind as in previous scenes. Shakespeare thus illustrates the love theme. The Duke is in the state of "loving" (in Gaylin's terms). He is not yet in the condition that Cesario perhaps represents.

Cesario presents more evidence that he is in touch with the reality of the situation. After the Duke requests that he go to Olivia to sue, Cesario counters with an eye-opening question: "But if she cannot love you, sir?" Not only does the Duke's answer suggest that his love continues intense, but it also demonstrates that love has a will of its own that may run at variance with reality. "No" is not a viable answer for him. In this way, Cesario is trying to reason with Orsino. Just because he is in love with Olivia, it doesn't follow that Olivia will fall in love with him.

The song Feste sings is prophetic, so it relates to the theme in a forward-looking manner. It expresses the death of love, which, in view of the Duke's confidence, may astonish the reader. The Duke feels that Olivia should reciprocate his love. But there's a song that tells of a "fair, cruel maid," who is obviously Olivia, who has killed her wooer. Cesario has already referred to Olivia as "fair cruelty." Olivia never accepts the love of Orsino. To the passionate lover, such rejection is tantamount to murder. So intense are the rejected lover's feelings that he desires to be buried in a grave. This intensity is fitting for Orsino, who has already expressed such passionate feelings for his beloved.

Study Questions

1. What is the first item the Duke requests?

2. Who is not immediately available to sing the song?

3. What kind of a lover does Orsino classify himself as?

4. What does the Duke surmise about Cesario?

5. According to the Duke, does the age of the man in a relationship matter?

6. What does the Clown's song focus on?

7. Who does the Clown insult?

8. Where does Cesario go once again?

9. What warning does Cesario give to Orsino about Olivia?

10. In what does the lover of the Clown's song wish to be laid?

Answers

1. The Duke requests some music.

2. The Clown is not immediately available to sing the song.

3. Orsino classifies himself as a "true lover."

4. The Duke surmises that Cesario has been in love.

5. Yes, the age of the male partner does matter.

6. The Clown's song focuses on the Duke's frustration with and subsequent failure to obtain Olivia.

7. The Clown insults the Duke.

8. Cesario goes to woo for the Duke.

9. Cesario warns the Duke that Olivia is not open to romance with him.

10. The lover is ready to be buried in a coffin.

Suggested Essay Topics

1. Analyze the song in this scene. Who and what is involved in it? Which *Twelfth Night* character does it relate to? Explain your answer.

2. Why does the Duke believe that the man should be older than the woman in a relationship? Consider his speech on page 26. Do you agree with his opinion? Why or why not?

Act II, Scene V (pages 29–34)

New Character:

Fabian: *the servant to Olivia who is the third spectator to Malvolio's humiliation*

Summary

This scene is devoted exclusively to the devious comic plot. Sir Toby gathers Fabian, another servant, and Andrew to enjoy the exercise in shame that Maria is about to execute. Fabian seems to have a bone to pick with him, so he is interested in what will happen to Malvolio.

Maria has the whole trick worked out. They will hide in a box tree and observe as Malvolio picks up the falsified letter to read it. Olivia is on Malvolio's mind when he enters. Sir Toby and Fabian believe that Malvolio's arrogance makes him suitable game for the trap that's been set. Malvolio fancies himself a suitor to Olivia.

Speaking aloud, Malvolio continues to let his imagination run wild over the prospect of loving Olivia and the accompanying self-aggrandizement. While doing so, Sir Toby, Fabian, and Andrew devilishly comment on his behavior. That they are sadistic in intention is evident in such remarks as "Pistol him, pistol him" and "O for a stone-bow, to hit him in the eye!"

Eventually Malvolio sees the letter, which appears to him to be in Olivia's handwriting. Though it is a love letter, it doesn't completely mention Malvolio by name. Malvolio takes the declaration of love to be addressed to him because it identifies the beloved as "M,O,A,I," four letters that can be found in Malvolio's name. Furthermore, the phrase "I may command where I adore" leads him to believe that he is the man because he is her servant.

The letter goes on to suggest that fortune is now smiling on Malvolio. The letter also induces him to adopt peculiar behaviors. He is to be hostile with a kinsman, smile in Olivia's presence, study political treatises for advice, and wear yellow stockings and cross-garters. Malvolio, convinced of the letter's authenticity, resolves to follow all of its suggestions.

Sir Toby foreshadows his subsequent marriage to Maria in this scene. He is so intrigued by her skill in the trap that he cannot help feeling love for her: "I could marry this wench for this device."

As yet, Malvolio has not humiliated himself before Olivia. The scheme will come to fruition when Malvolio confronts Olivia with smiles and yellow stockings, cross-gartered. So, for this devilish group, the best is yet to come.

Analysis

"Whether Malvolio has been most notoriously abused, or whether he is the well-deserving victim of a practical joke that explodes his vanity, social-climbing, and pretentiousness is the point at issue," says Maurice Charney. Until the device of Maria's letter, the play does not firmly emphasize Malvolio's vanity and social-climbing. As has been shown, he properly carries out his duty for Olivia. Only through what other characters say of him may we feel justified in labeling him an "overweening rogue," as Sir Toby does. His behavior, though, is quite proper.

What we should come to terms with is the relationship of this comic plot to the other plot. What it has in common, of course, is the theme of love. Malvolio is duped into believing that Olivia loves him, and he falls in love. This "symbolist drama," as Ralph Berry terms it, becomes a perversion of Orsino's love for Olivia. Malvolio may be likened to the Duke in the way that the letter ignites his passion for her. The letter, as a practical means of expression, reminds us of Cesario's position in the total rendering of the love theme. But, since the letter is a trick, Malvolio's love is a parody of the feelings and behavior of the Duke and Cesario. Olivia does not, nor will she, love Malvolio.

Perhaps the most glaring instance of perverseness is in the endings of the plots. Comedy prescribes a happy ending for the lovers in the romantic plot. Maria's contrived plot only issues forth a cruel outcome for Malvolio. The letter contains no truth. Malvolio will go mad.

This scheme is too cruel to be characterized as a bit of sport in keeping with the festive atmosphere. The desire for revenge that Sir Toby and Maria reveal undermines the acceptability of such as "jest," as Sir Toby euphemistically calls it. Malvolio is alienated from the rest of the household, and the way in which its members so handily trap him, "the woodcock near the gin," emphasizes his alienation. From the moment Malvolio enters, he is unaware of the others in the box tree. His lines are interspersed with the reactions of the spectators, with neither side being able to hear the other. This gives us a physical representation of the psychological phenomenon of "alienation." The spectators enjoy the device on Malvolio at the expense of his pride and feelings.

It is evident why this plot element in the play has been puzzling to critics.

The spectators to the trick associate animal imagery with Malvolio throughout this scene. This imagery lays emphasis on both his alienation from them as human beings and their view of him as an egotistical fool. Sir Toby's first question to Fabian refers to Malvolio as a "sheep-biter," that is, sneaky dog. To Maria, he is the "trout that must be caught with tickling." For Fabian, he is alternately a "rare turkey cock" and a "woodcock near the gin." Sir Toby also uses a bird image after Malvolio has begun reading the letter. As these characters delight in the cruel scheme, they feel that they have Malvolio right where they want him. Reducing Malvolio in their eyes to animal status sharply conveys that feeling. Animals lack reason, so they are wrapped up in their own little worlds to the extent that they operate by instincts. Sir Toby, Fabian, Andrew, and Maria are presumably drawing a parallel between the animals' instinctual selfishness and Malvolio's egoism.

Study Questions

1. Who is Fabian?

2. What is his motive for tricking Malvolio?

3. Who has worked out the scheme?

4. Where will the spectators of the device hide?

5. What does Malvolio fancy himself?

6. What kind of intention do Sir Toby and Andrew evidence by their remarks?

7. In whose handwriting supposedly is the letter that Malvolio finds?

8. What four letters in the letter lead Malvolio to believe it is addressed to him?

9. What is the source of imagery used by Sir Toby, Andrew, Maria, and Fabian to characterize Malvolio's situation?

10. From whom is Malvolio alienated?

Answers

1. Fabian is another of Olivia's servants.

2. Fabian apparently has a bone to pick with Malvolio.

3. Maria has worked out the scheme.

4. The spectators will hide in a box tree.

5. Malvolio fancies himself a suitor to Olivia.

6. Sir Toby and Andrew evidence a sadistic intention.

7. The letter is supposedly in Olivia's handwriting.

8. "M,O,A,I" lead Malvolio to believe it is addressed to him.

9. They use animal imagery to enlighten us about Malvolio's situation.

10. Malvolio is alienated from the rest of the household.

Suggested Essay Topics

1. Make the argument that Sir Toby, Andrew, Maria, and Fabian are behaving cruelly toward Malvolio. Is their cruelty justified in the light of the whole play? Do you personally accept the gulling of Malvolio?

2. Write an essay on "the love letter." First of all, define what you think it is. Does Maria's dropped letter fit your definition? What do you think of the requests made in the letter? How would you compose your own real love letter.

SECTION FOUR

Act III

Act III, Scene I (pages 34–39)

Summary

Cesario and Feste the Clown are conversing in Olivia's garden. Cesario, of course, has arrived with the purpose of courting Olivia. Cesario begins by asking the Clown if he earns a living with his tabor. In addition to engaging Cesario in wordplay, the Clown comments on the arbitrariness of words. People can do whatever they like with them regardless of good or bad intentions. Cesario briefly turns the conversation to identifying the fool. Feste, as usual, cannot give her a straight answer. He answers ironically that Olivia has no fool until she marries the man who will accept the role. In a short span, the Clown mentions a beard for Cesario, coins earning interest, and the love story of *Troilus and Cressida*. The Clown then goes to fetch Olivia. While awaiting Olivia, Cesario praises Feste's skillfulness at being a fool.

Sir Toby and Andrew arrive before Olivia. Sir Toby informs Cesario that Olivia is eager to see him. Paradoxically, Cesario asserts that he is Olivia's servant as well as Orsino's because the Duke has put himself at Olivia's service. His servant therefore is also hers. Olivia insists that she does not want to hear anymore wooing. Orsino is out.

Olivia, recalling the ring, broaches the subject of love toward Cesario. Cesario, rather than accept her love, says that he feels pity for Olivia. Cesario faithfully suggests the Duke's love again only to hear Olivia pour out her feelings of love for him: "I love thee so, that, maugre all thy pride,/Nor wit nor reason can my passion hide." Cesario does not wish to form a relationship with Olivia or any woman.

Analysis

We are meant to note a kind of kinship between Feste and Cesario. Shakespeare establishes this kinship by means of the ploce in the opening dialogue. For example, when Cesario says that those who manipulate words can make them "wanton," meaning equivocal, Feste picks up on another sense of "wanton," that is, unchaste, in his response. They have used the same word but in different senses. To play on someone else's words shows an interconnection between the two characters' ways of thinking. Cesario appreciates the Clown and even pays him for acting his role as fool.

The Clown of this play is a wordsmith and logician, in addition to being a good singer of the thematic songs. It behooves us to question the Clown's self-conscious commentary about words and their logic. He even refers to himself as not the fool, but rather Olivia's "corrupter of words." In essence, the Clown indicates his understanding of the arbitrariness of words: "Words are grown so false, I am loath to prove reason with them." There is no necessary and sufficient relationship between words and the reality to which they refer. Therefore, people can so manipulate words to do and say what they want, whether or not the words are true to the reality of the situation. Keeping in mind Cesario's connection with the motif of "appearances versus reality," his appreciation for the Clown's sensitivity to that issue is readily understandable. This scene sketches the Clown/fool's role in the play. For the characters in the play, this role of fool has entertainment value, and for the readers, his words have relevance to the play's interpretation.

In his short soliloquy following the Clown's departure, Cesario reveals his appreciation for the skill Feste exercises: "And to do that well craves a kind of wit." If Cesario can appreciate this skill, he is certainly capable of exercising it himself. The Clown is attuned to the mood and quality of people with whom he practices his fooling. Although we can assert that the Clown is very talented in his use of words, the truth value of what he says about others is not so clear.

Cesario, who represents practical common sense for the lovers, is everywhere a most admirable character. He makes a diligent effort to woo on Orsino's behalf. Another way that Shakespeare demonstrates his good communication skills is in the way he uses the same metaphors as other characters. When Sir Toby uses a trade metaphor, "trade be to," to characterize Cesario's presence in the garden, Cesario responds with another expression drawn from the language of trade, "I am bound to your niece." Cesario understands and can get along with all the characters in the play.

Olivia discloses her love for Cesario in this scene. The fundamental irony is that Cesario is there on the Duke's behalf, but Olivia expresses love for Cesario. This creates a complication in the original plot. Not only has Olivia not reciprocated her love to Orsino, but she's also bestowed it on Cesario. At this point, although we should expect a happy resolution to this entanglement, the issue of who-joins-who is not clear in this scene. Olivia, in declaring her love, is in the state of "loving": Cesario does not accept her offer.

The one clue we have that Cesario cannot wind up with Olivia is the knowledge of his true gender. Cesario is really a woman, so he must be paired with a male. At this point, we can surmise that Cesario will form a relationship with Orsino, the man for whom his female self has already expressed an attraction. Herschel Baker argues that the delay in the happy ending derives from the characters' inability to know the truth about themselves. This brings in the issue of "self-knowledge." Not everyone knows who they are, what they believe, or what they really want out of life. Thus, Cesario's disguise represents any such intellectual and emotional confusion of the other characters in concrete terms. It is only when he unmasks at the end and the misconception is cleared up that they can feel a sense of liberation from their illusions. Self-knowledge is attained, according to this view. This view changes Cesario's place in the love theme.

Taking the plunge into the experience of love, as Orsino and Olivia amply demonstrate, appears easy enough. The important related step of cementing a bond between the two persons is not so easy. Understanding this truism makes Cesario an appealing and curious character in the play.

Study Questions

1. What instrument is the Clown holding?

2. Where does the Clown say he lives by?

3. Why is the Clown upset with words?

4. Rather than Lady Olivia's fool, what does Feste claim to be?

5. What does Cesario praise while waiting for Olivia?

6. Who declares love in this scene?

7. What is Olivia's response to Cesario's wooing for the Duke?

8. Between what two characters does Shakespeare establish a kinship?

9. What happens when wise men act foolishly?

10. According to Herschel Baker, what do the characters lack?

Answers

1. The Clown is holding a tabor.

2. The Clown says he lives by a church.

3. The Clown is upset with words because they are rascals whose bonds disgraced them.

4. Feste claims to be Olivia's "corrupter of words."

5. Cesario praises the Clown's skill as a fool.

6. Olivia declares her love for Cesario in this scene.

7. Olivia rejects the Duke.

8. Shakespeare establishes a kinship between Cesario and the Clown.

9. They betray their common sense.

10. The characters lack self-knowledge.

Suggested Essay Topics

1. Describe the way in which the Clown carries out his role as "fool." What functions does he see himself as performing?

Does he fulfill them as he thinks he should? Make a judgment at the end of your essay as to whether he is a necessary or superfluous character in the play.

2. As Olivia is in the process of revealing her feelings for Cesario, she makes use of metaphors drawn from the animal kingdom (bottom of page 37 and top of page 38). State what these animal metaphors are, and then explain their significance. How do they illuminate the depth of Olivia's feelings at the moment?

Act III, Scene II (pages 39–41)

Summary

Sir Andrew is disappointed that Olivia has not shown an interest in him. He has seen her giving more attention to Cesario than to him. Fabian claims that Olivia was deliberately trying to exasperate Andrew so as to spur him to more aggressive action. Andrew should have seized the moment to prove his masculinity: "You should have banged the youth into dumbness." Having failed to act has put Andrew way out of Olivia's thoughts, unless he can act quickly to arouse her admiration with his valor. Andrew agrees.

Sir Toby's idea for Andrew to achieve Olivia's love is to challenge Cesario to a fight. A fight will kindle her admiration. Sir Toby tells Andrew to write out a provocative challenge—"Let there be gall enough in thy ink"—to Cesario. Despite this incitement, Sir Toby says he will not actually deliver the letter to the youth.

Sir Toby espies Maria with a term of affection. Maria informs them how hilarious Malvolio's deception has turned out. He has obeyed every point of the letter. She manifests her sadistic pleasure in the way he is so taken over by the letter.

Analysis

Sir Toby plays his role as "lord of misrule" in this scene as well as in others. No sooner has Sir Andrew conveyed his frustration at winning Olivia's hand than does Toby devise a hostile plan to get her attention. It might be more proper to designate someone to court Olivia, as Cesario has done for Orsino, But, he instead tells Sir Andrew to write an inflammatory letter to Cesario, a letter Sir Toby does not intend to pass on. Sir Toby keeps the action lively, stirring up a fracas that has love as its dubious impetus.

Sir Toby's plan reveals, moreover, underlying masculine values. First of all, he proposes a fight, which is often considered a manly activity. Secondly, he and Fabian place a great value on "valor" as a stimulus to love. This statement of belief in valor as a "lovebroker" for Sir Andrew is more evidence of the breadth of the love theme. Love is very subjective. People may love another for varied reasons and in varying intensities. In Sir Toby's masculine world, the reputation of valor may lead a woman into love.

Maria comes in to report that her scheme is reaching its high point. She deems it odd that Malvolio has so naively accepted the contents of the letter to the point of following every item. She mentions the confrontation with Olivia that is about to take place. However perverse it may be, Malvolio's embarrassing descent into love is also indicative of the subjective nature of the experience of love. It's puzzling, however, why Malvolio was so ripe to fall for his lady—unless the reader accepts the argument that Malvolio is egotistical and arrogant.

Study Questions

1. What is Sir Andrew getting ready to do?
2. On whom does Andrew see Olivia bestow her affection?
3. What is Fabian's explanation for that favoritism?
4. What element does Fabian think will stir Olivia's passion?
5. What idea does Sir Toby come up with to help Sir Andrew?
6. What task does Sir Toby assign Sir Andrew?
7. What does Sir Toby not plan to do, though?
8. In what manner does Sir Toby hail Maria?

9. How does Maria describe Malvolio's absorption in the letter?

10. What role does Sir Toby continue to play well?

Answers

1. Sir Andrew is getting ready to leave.

2. Andrew sees Olivia bestow her affection on Cesario.

3. Fabian asserts that she is doing that to exasperate Andrew and to rouse him to some action.

4. Fabian thinks that valor will stir Olivia to passion.

5. Sir Toby comes up with the idea of a fight.

6. Sir Toby assigns a letter to Sir Andrew to be delivered to Cesario.

7. Sir Toby does not plan to deliver the letter.

8. Sir Toby hails Maria in an affectionate manner.

9. Maria describes Malvolio's absorption in the letter as hilarious.

10. Sir Toby continues to play the role of "lord of misrule" well.

Suggested Essay Topics

1. Articulate Fabian and Sir Toby's assumption about the strength of a man's valor in inciting love. Then write an opinion essay on whether you think valor, "machoness," manliness, etc. are all that are necessary to win a woman's love. Are they sound bases to build a love on? Explain your thesis.

2. Summarize briefly all the love connections up to this point. Even sound like a gossip. Tell who loves who and who has hopes of who. Then, in the remainder of the essay, explain who you think deserves to be together with whom. In other words, you be the matchmaker. (You don't have to agree with Shakespeare's resolution of the complications.)

Act III, Scene III (pages 41–43)

Summary

This short scene lets us know that Sebastian and Antonio are making their way into the action; they have not been left out. Antonio explains to a grateful Sebastian that both love and concern for his safety urged him to catch up to the youth. Antonio knows the area; Sebastian does not.

Sebastian desires to do some sightseeing in town, to see the "memorials and the things of fame," but Antonio has to back out. Antonio is wanted by Orsino's court for his part in a previous incident at sea. Sebastian reckons that perhaps he has murdered. Not so; Antonio says he is only guilty of piracy.

Antonio gives his money to Sebastian in case he wishes to purchase something, while Antonio lays low. He also recommends an inn where they can meet (the Elephant). They agree to find each other there.

Analysis

This scene does advance the plot even though there is no mention of either character's being in love. Sebastian is Viola's twin brother. As far as the love theme is concerned, we can predict—since a theme should be coherently worked out—that just as Viola has a place in the love plot, so too will Sebastian. He is a missing link. Olivia, Orsino, and Cesario expressing love make an uneven number. One more is needed to make two couples. These two couples, as they will eventually turn out to be, constitute two of the three love knots that are realized by the end of the play. Malvolio's love comes to naught, however, and Sir Andrew never gets Olivia.

We have had plenty of exposure to Olivia, Orsino, and Cesario's brand of loving and being loved in the play. So, Shakespeare need not belabor the role that Cesario has represented as the practical, commonsense-oriented person in the relationship. It's the Cesarios that keep the relationship going from day to day. The family tie that exists between Viola and Sebastian also implies a thematic parallel between the two characters. Shakespeare's economy had no need to dramatize Sebastian's practicality.

Antonio is familiar with the Duke and his Illyria. He, unfortunately, has had a run-in with the Duke's men in the past, so he feels it necessary to hide his presence. Shakespeare keeps him involved in the plot in such a way that will call attention to the illusion created by Viola's disguise. Later on, Antonio will take Cesario for Sebastian.

Study Questions

1. What does Sebastian say he will not do to Antonio?
2. Where do they meet?
3. What encouraged Antonio to keep up with Sebastian?
4. How does Antonio describe the area they're in?
5. What does Sebastian desire to do in Illyria?
6. Why does Antonio have to decline Sebastian's offer to see the town?
7. What does Sebastian reckon Antonio has done?
8. What does Antonio say he is guilty of?
9. Who is the missing link in the love strands?
10. With what character does Sebastian have a similar thematic function?

Answers

1. Sebastian says he will not chide him.
2. They meet in a street.
3. Antonio's love and concern for Sebastian encouraged him to keep up.
4. Antonio describes the area as "rough and unhospitable."
5. Sebastian desires to go sightseeing.
6. Antonio has to decline Sebastian's offer to accompany him because he is a wanted man.
7. Sebastian reckons Antonio has murdered.
8. Antonio says he is guilty of piracy.

9. Antonio is the missing link in the love strands.

10. Sebastian and Viola have similar thematic functions.

Suggested Essay Topics

1. Why doesn't Antonio find love in this play? Is it because a play can only have so many major and minor characters? Does he deserve to be matched up with Olivia, Viola, or some other woman in Illyria?

2. How does Shakespeare render the relationship between Antonio and Sebastian? Compare their relationship to Sir Toby and Sir Andrew's. Discuss the importance of friendship in a play like *Twelfth Night*.

Act III, Scene IV (pages 43–53)

New Characters:

Servant: *the one who informs Olivia of Cesario's return*

First Officer: *one of the Duke's officials who comes to arrest Antonio*

Second Officer: *accompanies the First Officer to carry out the arrest*

Summary

Olivia, longing for Cesario and out of sorts, wonders where Malvolio is. Here, she commends his nature as agreeable to her. Maria alerts her to his agitated state: "He is, sure, possessed." In accordance with the letter, Malvolio is smiling about the place. Nonetheless, Olivia wants to see him because she feels as disturbed as he.

Malvolio speaks to Olivia as though she knew about the letter. His smiling doesn't fit the mood Olivia is in. After Malvolio refers to his cross-gartering, Olivia asks if there is something wrong. Malvolio only mentions the commands of the letter to explain his behavior. For the rest of the dialogue between them, Malvolio quotes directly from Maria's letter, while Olivia intersperses her bewildered replies. Having been subjected to this unaccountable behavior, Olivia considers Malvolio to be mad: "Why, this is very midsummer madness." At this point, a servant enters with news that Cesario has come.

In his soliloquy, Malvolio sounds convinced that Olivia is following the letter. So, her bewilderment was lost on him as he raved on. He thanks Jove for the divine assistance he's been given.

Sir Toby, along with Fabian and Maria, comes to investigate Malvolio's behavior. Malvolio assumes the hostility toward him that the letter commands, not listening to the mock sympathy Sir Toby demonstrates. Fabian and Maria's similarly mock sympathy must be false because they know he's still under the influence of the letter. When Malvolio leaves, the culprits reflect on Malvolio's absorption by the letter. Sir Toby foreshadows at Malvolio's madness and ordeal in the dark room.

Sir Andrew enters with his letter of challenge. Fabian compliments the phrasing of the letter, containing a challenge to a fight, as Sir Toby reads it aloud. Sir Andrew is then egged on to draw on Cesario in the orchard. Claiming that Sir Andrew's letter will not ring true for Cesario, Sir Toby chooses to convey the challenge by word of mouth in order to "drive the gentleman...into a most hideous opinion of his rage, skill, fury, and impetuosity."

Following this, there is a brief interlude involving Olivia and Cesario. Olivia complains that her protestations of love are falling on deaf ears. Part of her thinks that it is blameworthy to be so bold, but another part of her holds that love gives her the freedom to speak her love. Cesario likens Olivia's passion to Orsino's. Giving Cesario a jewel, Olivia asks him to return tomorrow. Olivia, conscious of her honor, wonders what it will inspire her to give Cesario. Cesario wants nothing but her return of love to the Duke. That is not possible for Olivia because she's given her love to Cesario. Olivia repeats her request for Cesario to come tomorrow.

When Olivia departs, Sir Toby alarms Cesario with the news that Sir Andrew is preparing to attack him. He urges Cesario to prepare to defend himself. Innocently Cesario cannot believe that he's done offense to anyone. Sir Toby counters that he has given cause for a fight. Sir Toby further tries to frighten Cesario with

Sir Andrew's strength and prowess. Sir Toby conjures an image of Sir Andrew as a valiant and well-connected knight who has three deaths in dueling to his credit. Cesario refuses to fight, it's not his way. So he seeks an escort from Lady Olivia.

Cesario surmises that Sir Andrew is only trying to test his valor. But Sir Toby explains that he has just cause. Cesario therefore must face the challenge. At Cesario's request, Sir Toby leaves to get Sir Andrew so he can tell him what offense Cesario has done. Fabian only admits to knowing that Sir Andrew is incensed against him. Fabian echoes Sir Toby's spurious praise of Sir Andrew's skill and power.

When Sir Toby finds Andrew, he scares him with an equally spurious account of Cesario's skill at fencing. Likewise, Andrew decides to avoid the duel, even offering his horse as a peace offering. Sir Toby supposedly rides off to make the proposal to Cesario. Cesario and Andrew are holding images of each other's hostility.

As these two men finally come together, Sir Toby alters the situation by claiming the cause not to be as grave as it was first thought to be. But, as a formality, they should have a duel. Sir Toby assures both of them that harm will not come of it.

After they draw, Antonio makes a timely entrance into the garden. His first impulse is to protect Cesario, who he believes is Sebastian. As soon as Sir Toby draws on Antonio, the Duke's officers enter. They recognize Antonio and arrest him. Antonio asks Cesario for some of the money he gave Sebastian. Cesario, though confused at this request (not being Sebastian), offers Antonio some of his own money. Antonio takes that as a denial and warns him that he will become angry at his ingratitude. Cesario affirms that Antonio is a stranger to him; Antonio cannot possibly hold a claim on him. Antonio recounts how he rescued Sebastian from drowning and showed him brotherly love. Antonio, feeling betrayed, leaves with the officers.

Cesario gathers that Antonio was referring to her brother, Sebastian. Realizing that he closely resembles his brother, Cesario fervently hopes that Antonio meant Sebastian.

Sir Toby judges Cesario a coward. This stirs up Sir Andrew's ire to fight, which is met with Sir Toby's command to give him a good thwacking.

Analysis

This is a lengthy scene in which Shakespeare draws together some of the loose ends of the love plot. Considering that Sebastian's presence is now signaled, this scene becomes the climax of the rising action. This revelation constitutes the major surprise, for the rest of the scene forms a logical continuation of plots that have been in motion since Act I. "This scene as a whole," according to L.G. Salingar, "with its rapid changes of mood and action, from Olivia to the subplot and back towards Sebastian, braces together the whole comic design."

In order for Malvolio's humiliation to be complete, he has to face Olivia under the influence of the letter. Olivia, at the start of the scene, has her mind on Cesario. She wants to see him and considers how she can best allure him. She speaks solemnly of Malvolio, "he is sad and civil," with whom she desires some fellowship. Maria alerts her to his mental agitation.

Malvolio's dialogue with Olivia is at once comic and perverse. We must laugh at the way he has been so duped by the other characters, as well as the way he carries the illusion until he is undeceived. The perversion of the love experience stands out prominently. Malvolio has the commands of the letter on his mind as he speaks to Olivia. Such love has no genuine source, as Orsino and Olivia's does. Malvolio elaborates on a love that Olivia has no idea of, nor has she any intention of falling in love with her servant. The only genuine element in this whole perverse matter is Malvolio's temporary infatuation. Shakespeare heightens the cruelty of the trick by having Maria play dumb and Olivia bespeak concern for his state of mind. Charles T. Prouty sums it up this way: "Thus the subplot may be seen as representing the obverse, the other side of the coin. In the main plot the characters move in the world of an established convention while in the other the characters are alien, if not antithetical, to the convention."

Sir Andrew returns to show Sir Toby the letter he has written. Sir Andrew has obviously taken a liking to Olivia; we have just not heard him utter his passion. Sir Toby's commonsense plan to interest Olivia in his friend partakes too much of the playful spirit of the play to qualify as reasonable interceding. Nonetheless, Sir Toby as the "lord of misrule" brings together these two major aspects of the play, love and foolery. Those two aspects intersect in the duel scene.

The interlude between Cesario and Olivia keeps their two distinct roles in the play sharply focused. The dialogue does not surprise us, so we can take pleasure in Cesario's consistency as representative of a practical quality. Olivia says that she has poured out her heart to a heart of stone. Cesario asserts his master's love, thus finely playing his role of intermediary.

In addition to blending the play's two key elements, the arranged fight between Cesario and Sir Andrew prepares the way for Antonio's timely rescue. Antonio comes upon the duel and believes he is saving his friend Sebastian. Regardless of whether the officers had come for him or not, it is evident that he would have made Sebastian's existence known. Upon his arrest, Antonio asks of Cesario the money he had given to Sebastian. The interchange that ensues finally brings out the name "Sebastian." Cesario's hope for her brother is revived.

Study Questions

1. How is Olivia feeling at the opening of the scene?

2. What does Olivia commend about Malvolio?

3. What influence sways Malvolio's mind as he speaks with Olivia?

4. In what words does Malvolio try to dismiss Sir Toby when he enters?

5. What does Sir Toby indicate his attitude toward Malvolio will be when the trick is done?

6. What does Sir Andrew return with?

7. How receptive is Cesario to Olivia's love?

8. With what news does Sir Toby alarm Cesario?

9. What does the knowledge of Sebastian's existence make of this scene?

10. How can we characterize Malvolio's dialogue with Olivia?

Answers

1. Olivia is out of sorts.

2. Olivia commends Malvolio's nature.

3. The commands of the letter sway Malvolio's mind as he speaks with Olivia.

4. Malvolio tries to dismiss Sir Toby with "Go off; I discard you."

5. Sir Toby indicates that he will show mercy on Malvolio when the trick is done.

6. Sir Andrew returns with the letter he wrote.

7. Cesario is not receptive to Olivia's love.

8. Sir Toby alarms Cesario with the report that Sir Andrew is preparing to attack him.

9. Knowledge of Sebastian's existence makes this a climactic scene.

10. We can characterize Malvolio's dialogue with Olivia as comic and perverse.

Suggested Essay Topics

1. Some critics have argued that Malvolio is presumptuous and arrogant. Discuss the extent to which those character-istics are responsible for his gulling and eventual madness. Support your case with evidence from the text.

2. Analyze this play in terms of its credibility and realism. To what extent is the action credible? To what extent is it fan-tasy and romance? Define the concepts you work with in your essay.

SECTION FIVE

Act IV

Act IV, Scene I (pages 53–55)

Summary

The Clown and Sebastian are talking in front of Olivia's house. Sebastian, unlike his sister, has not taken so well to Feste. They seem at odds with each other. Sebastian dismisses the Clown, maintaining that he has no business with him. The Clown, characteristically clever, responds by denying the reality of everything: "Nothing that is so is so." Indeed, Sebastian is not Cesario. Sebastian orders Feste to take his folly elsewhere. The Clown, clever though he be, is not omniscient, so he thinks that Sebastian is just pretending ignorance. He requests a message for Olivia. Sebastian dismisses him with an insult, but not without giving him a tip. The Clown is thankful.

Sir Andrew, Sir Toby, and Fabian enter. Sir Andrew immediately strikes Sebastian, mistaking him for Cesario. Though puzzled, Sebastian strikes multiple blows in return. Sir Toby joins the fray to help Sir Andrew by seizing Sebastian. After witnessing the fray, the Clown goes off to inform Olivia.

They continue the fight, with Sir Andrew threatening legal action and Sebastian ordering them to let go. Sebastian forcefully disentangles himself from their holds and warns them that on further provocation, he'll draw his sword. Apparently, Sir Toby cannot resist; he draws on Sebastian.

Olivia enters and surveys the scene to her distaste. The fracas is yet another instance of Sir Toby's uncivilized tastes. She orders them to stop and get out. That her beloved (or the one she thinks is Cesario) is involved in the fight adds to her sense of offense. Olivia hopes that Sebastian will look rationally on the incident. She invites him to her house so she can tell him about Sir Toby's other "fruitless pranks."

Olivia's invitation baffles Sebastian. He wishes for further oblivion to add to the confusion he is experiencing. Yet, when Olivia repeats her invitation, he accepts.

Analysis

Critics disagree on how to interpret Feste's role. Despite Sebastian's attitude to Feste, the Clown and his role retain their dignity within the play. If anything, Sebastian depreciates the value of the Clown's content, that is, what it is he talks about. Cesario's praise for his wit, however, is well-taken. And his wit is clever in this scene. Although the Clown's songs have relevance to the theme and plot, the relevance of his dialogue is less clear. He is good with words and logic, and his displays of skill have proven quite entertaining, but whether he penetrates character and motive remains debatable. After all, in reality, Sebastian is not dissembling. Feste does not know he's with Sebastian instead of Cesario. L.G. Salingar puts it this way, "Feste is not the ringleader in *Twelfth Night*, nor is he exactly the play's philosopher." Similarly, Maurice Charney, in his chapter on *Twelfth Night*, discusses only Feste's agile mind at wordplay.

This is the scene in which Sebastian and Olivia are brought together, the foursome of the love plot is hence complete. Rightly so, the confusion seems all on Sebastian's part.

> What relish is in this? how runs the stream?
> Or I am mad, or else this is a dream:
> Let fancy still my sense in Lethe steep;
> If it be thus to dream, still let me sleep! (page 55)

This confusion arises out of the familiar way in which Olivia addresses Sebastian, whom she thinks is Cesario. Olivia has had dealings with Cesario already and expressed her love for him. In this scene, since they are twins, she thinks it is he. Sebastian does not fall in love with Olivia; rather, he puzzles over her familiarity. What does she mean, he wonders. The whole situation seems so unreal that he thinks he may have lost his senses. Yet he goes along with Olivia, perhaps taking pleasure in the illusion. He asks for oblivion so he can prolong the dream that Olivia is sustaining. To the extent that Sebastian's analogous role (to his sister's) is a necessary component to the love theme, his acquiescence in Olivia's dream is very likely. One of the complications of the plot is about to be cleared up, and the genre's happy ending is happily in the offing.

Study Questions

1. How does Sebastian react to Feste?

2. What does Sebastian tell the Clown to vent elsewhere?

3. Who tells the other to abandon his pretense?

4. Who fights in this scene?

5. When the Clown sees the fray, what does he do?

6. Who breaks up the fight?

7. How does Olivia characterize Sir Toby's behavior?

8. To whom does Olivia issue an invitation?

9. How does Sebastian respond to Olivia's invitation?

10. What does Maurice Charney say about Feste's mind?

Answers

1. Sebastian dismisses the Clown.

2. Sebastian tells the Clown to vent his folly elsewhere.

3. Feste tells Sebastian to abandon his pretense, "ungird thy strangeness."

4. Sebastian, Sir Andrew, and Sir Toby fight in this scene.

5. The Clown goes off to inform Olivia.

6. Olivia breaks up the fight.

7. Olivia calls Sir Toby a "rudesby" and "ungracious wretch."

8. Olivia issues an invitation to Sebastian.

9. Sebastian is surprised at Olivia's invitation.

10. Maurice Charney says that Feste has an "agile mind at wordplay."

Suggested Essay Topics

1. In what way do Viola–Sebastian constitute a "poetic symbol," as one critic has said. In other words, if they are one spirit in two bodies, how does that technique help us to understand Shakespeare's vision of love in the play? Be careful to explain the symbolism before you construct your argument.

2. Discuss Olivia's attitude toward the brawl she comes upon. Find other places in the play where Sir Toby's foolery is criticized and list them. Why do you think characters express disapproval for the festive behavior? How would the play stand without Sir Toby's merriment?

Act IV, Scene II (pages 55–58)

Summary

Maria gives the Clown a gown and beard, apparently wishing to prolong the sham with Malvolio. Feste readily accepts the offer to play Chaucer's Sir Topas. He has a stereotyped notion of a curate and a student, which he doesn't fit, though he does account himself an honest man and a good citizen. Sir Toby enters, greeting him as a parson, and pushes him on to Malvolio.

The Clown, dressed as Sir Topas, visits Malvolio in a very dark room. Malvolio immediately orders Sir Topas to go to Olivia without specifying the contents of his message. Malvolio perceives himself as a wronged man. He says that to Sir Topas and, in the same breath, he asserts his sanity. Sir Topas responds with assurance of his own mildness. Malvolio insists that the house is dark and that his abusers have laid him in the darkness. Sir Topas points out that there are sources of light coming into the room. Malvolio suggests that it's perhaps a figurative darkness surrounding him as well as maintaining his sanity once again. Sir Topas does not admit to any darkness, insinuating instead that Malvolio is full of perplexity.

Malvolio asks for a test of his sanity, to which Sir Topas responds with a question about Pythagoras' doctrine. Malvolio answers aptly, but Sir Topas does not admit his sanity.

According to Maria, Malvolio is so blinded he cannot even see the Clown's disguise. The Clown goes once more, at Sir Toby's prompting, to talk with Malvolio. Sir Toby shows that his sadism in the matter has not subsided. The reason he must stop the trick is Olivia's disapproval of his antics.

The second conversation between Malvolio and Sir Topas follows in the same vein as the previous one. This time, Malvolio requests a pen, ink, and paper with which he can write to Olivia. The Clown (as Sir Topas) persists in the contention that Malvolio is mad, which Malvolio vigorously rejects. Moreover, Malvolio's counterclaim of abuse in this scene provides compelling evidence of the validity of his perceptions. He has indeed been played with.

During this conversation, the Clown speaks to Malvolio as both the Clown and Sir Topas. When Malvolio realizes this, he asks the Clown to get him some paper and light. He wants to send a message to Olivia. The Clown, though agreeing to help, still cannot resist implying that Malvolio is mad.

The Clown ends this scene with a song, whose significance is a bit obscure but does bear relevance to Malvolio's present predicament.

Analysis

The Clown puts on an act in this scene. He goes to Malvolio's room disguised as a Chaucerian curate, Sir Topas. This performance is commendable to the extent that the Clown is fulfilling his role as jester. It is truly his role to entertain the others. The talent the Clown exhibits is also impressive. It is not easy to do all that he does in this play.

Maria shows that she wants to antagonize Malvolio and continue the cruel deception. The Clown operates more out of the requirements of his role than a desire to further vex Malvolio.

What he says to Malvolio helps to illuminate Malvolio's character and the effect of the trick on him. Malvolio is certain that he has been wronged. The confidence with which he asserts the abuse builds our sympathy for him. He appears the undeserving victim of a cruel hoax. A man who can perceive the wickedness of abuse would probably not be the kind to foist abuse on others. His perception therefore is valid.

The Clown insinuates that he is mad. Malvolio maintains his sanity. His perception of his sanity is reinforced by his desire to communicate with Olivia. He knows he has humiliated himself before her, and the reasonable thing to do is to make amends. The impulse to communicate is a sound one. Presumably he wants to apologize and to show her that he is in possession of his faculties.

The darkness surrounding Malvolio symbolizes his alienation from the other members of the household, which has reached a grotesque level. The darkness also suggests more. It may symbolize the cruelty and lack of understanding of the other characters. They are the ones who have abused him as he eloquently maintains. The Clown points out that there are sources of light in the room. They just aren't illuminating a man who has been swooped down on by malicious associates. The darkness may symbolize the closedmindedness of the Puritans. His incarceration may be the "lack of freedom" of the Puritanical philosophy.

The image of darkness coupled with allusions to the Devil offer compelling evidence of bad intentions on the other characters' parts and Malvolio's sound character. Sir Topas' second speech to Malvolio reflects this: "Out hyperbolical fiend! how vexest thou this man!" Sir Topas states explicitly that the forces impinging on Malvolio are malicious.

Study Questions

1. What two articles does Maria give the Clown?

2. Whom does she want Feste to play?

3. What label does Sir Topas greet Malvolio with?

4. What kind of room is Malvolio in?

5. What are the two sources of light in that room?

6. How does Malvolio perceive himself?

7. What items does Malvolio request from Sir Topas?

8. What kind of test does Malvolio ask for?

9. Why does Sir Toby feel compelled to put a stop to the trick?

10. What image in the scene suggests the cruelty of Maria and Sir Toby?

Answers

1. Maria gives the Clown a gown and a beard.

2. Maria wants Feste to play Sir Topas.

3. Sir Topas greets Malvolio as "Malvolio the lunatic."

4. Malvolio is in a very dark room.

5. The two sources of light in the room are bay windows and clerestories.

6. Malvolio perceives himself as a wronged man.

7. Malvolio requests a candle, pen, ink, and paper from Sir Topas.

8. Malvolio asks for a test of his sanity.

9. Sir Toby feels compelled to put a stop to the trick because Olivia disapproves of his nonsense.

10. The darkness image suggests the cruelty of Maria and Sir Toby.

Suggested Essay Topics

1. Why does the Clown insist that Malvolio is mad? Whom do you believe, Malvolio or Sir Topas/Clown? If Malvolio is not mad, in your opinion, what does the Clown's insistence suggest about his role in the play? If Malvolio is mad, explain why you don't accept his contentions.

2. Analyze the song with which the Clown closes the scene.

ACT IV, SCENE II

Is the allusion to the Devil in harmony with the preceding allusions in the scene? How does the song pass judgment on Malvolio?

Act IV, Scene III (pages 58–59)

Summary

This scene is set in the garden, a fitting locale for the culmination of a love match. Sebastian tries to come to terms with his good luck in his opening soliloquy. This love match is so quick that we have no inkling as to Sebastian's feelings about love as an experience and as they relate to Olivia.

He tells us that she gave him a pearl. He marvels at his new-found sweetheart and discounts that he is mad. He wishes for Antonio, who he couldn't locate at the Elephant, and for his esteemed advice. The improbability of his good fortune leads him to doubt the reality of what has happened. Unlike Cesario, however, he doesn't reject Olivia's gift of love. When the thought crosses his mind that Olivia may be mad, he dispels it immediately with the knowledge that Olivia is such a competent and fit manager of the affairs of her household. His good instincts conclude that there's some kind of deception attaching to Olivia's love.

Olivia wastes no time in proposing marriage. She has brought a priest to Sebastian to marry them. She invites Sebastian to the nearby chapel to participate in the ceremony. She promises him confidentiality until such time as he becomes ready to divulge the news of their wedlock. Sebastian accepts, pledging his everlasting faithfulness.

Analysis

In this scene, one of the love matches is fully realized. Olivia and Sebastian marry. This is a hasty move for Sebastian, who accepts, but not for Olivia. She has been in love with his twin (Cesario) throughout the play. So, she feels a sense of triumph in gaining her beloved. Sebastian, on the other hand, should express the surprise and wonder that he does. The play hitherto has given us little knowledge of his thoughts and feelings.

Sebastian's significance resides in his symbolic function as Viola's thematic twin.

Sebastian and Olivia serve to illustrate the love theme quite well. Olivia has expressed her love; Sebastian takes his place as the practical, common sense complement to the loving aspect. His soliloquy reflects his appreciation for the role of reason and prudent management in life. He praises Olivia for the latter.

Study Questions

1. Why is the garden an appropriate setting for this scene?
2. What does Sebastian try to come to terms with?
3. What does the rapidity of the love match prevent us from obtaining?
4. What gift has Olivia given Sebastian?
5. Whom does Sebastian wish to speak with?
6. Does he accept or reject Olivia's love?
7. What skill of Olivia's does Sebastian praise?
8. What plans has Olivia made?
9. Who has she brought to carry out those plans?
10. What is the key symbolic element of this scene?

Answers

1. It is appropriate because a wedding is about to take place.
2. Sebastian tries to come to terms with his good luck.
3. The rapidity of the love match prevents us from obtaining Sebastian's feelings about love.
4. Olivia gives Sebastian a pearl.
5. Sebastian wishes to speak with Antonio.
6. He accepts Olivia's love.
7. Sebastian praises Olivia's management of affairs in the house.
8. Olivia has planned a wedding ceremony.

9. She has brought a priest to tie the knot.

10. The key symbolic element is the twins.

Suggested Essay Topics

1. What is an "arranged marriage"? Do you know of anyone who was part of an arrangement? What motives may be involved? Compare an arranged marriage to the manner in which Sebastian and Olivia are brought together.

2. Consider the influence of "accident and flood of fortune" on Sebastian's success with Olivia. Is the marriage just good luck and is Sebastian taking advantage of an opportunity to marry up? Discuss Sebastian's attitude to Olivia in your essay.

SECTION SIX

Act V

Act V, Scene I (pages 60–71)

Summary

This scene forms a conglomeration of previous elements in the play. We are before Olivia's house when it opens with Fabian and the Clown. Fabian is asking Feste to show him Malvolio's letter to Olivia, which he doesn't want to show him.

After this brief exchange, the Duke, Cesario, Curio, and other lords are on the scene. After inquiring of Feste and Fabian if they are connected to Olivia, the Duke recognizes one of them as the Clown. Upon being asked how he is, the Clown starts in with his wordplay. He answers ironically that, as far as his foes are concerned, he is better, and as far as his friends are concerned, he is worse. That makes no sense to the Duke, so he requests an explanation. The Clown's explanation holds that friends deceive, while enemies tell the cold truth. Once explained, the Duke likes the idea and tips him. The Clown wants more and gets another coin from the Duke. Before leaving to summon Olivia, the Clown requests yet another coin from the Duke.

Antonio and the officers then enter. Cesario recognizes Antonio as the man who stepped in on his fight with Sir Andrew. The Duke also recognizes Antonio from the time when he did courageous battle with one of his ships. An officer relates that he arrested Antonio while fighting in the street. Cesario hastens to his defense mentioning his help, though his speech quite perplexed him.

ACT V, SCENE I

Antonio recounts how he saved Sebastian, inadvertently referring to Cesario, and offered his love and service to him. He exposed himself to danger for Sebastian's sake. Yet, Sebastian denied him when he intervened in the fight. Sebastian held back his purse, too.

Cesario wonders how that could be possible. He has been under the Duke's service since arriving in Illyria.

In walks Olivia asking the Duke how she can be of service to him. She takes Cesario for Sebastian. Olivia's speech thus baffles Cesario. Olivia repeats her rejection of the Duke. The Duke expresses his disappointment and adds a fierce note for emphasis. He retaliates by spiriting Cesario away, out of Olivia's sight. Cesario, supportive of the Duke, reveals his love for him.

Olivia calls for the priest to remind Cesario that they are married. She thinks that Cesario is afraid to admit the truth. The priest comes to substantiate the marital bond that exists between them (her and Sebastian). This proof convinces the Duke, who becomes angry with Cesario.

Sir Andrew, entering injured, calls for a doctor to attend him and Sir Toby. Sir Andrew lays the blame for this violence on Cesario. Cesario, of course, denies the charge. Sir Andrew was set on him by Sir Toby. Sir Toby enters limping and requests a doctor. Olivia orders him to bed.

Sebastian enters with an apology for the injuries he has produced. He was justified inasmuch as he acted in self-defense. The Duke notices the resemblance between him and Cesario, considering it an optical illusion. Sebastian is glad to see Antonio.

For the first time in the play, Sebastian speaks to Cesario. Cesario offers clear proof that he and Sebastian are related. The time is not right for Cesario to unmask, but he promises to bring Sebastian to where his woman's clothes are hidden.

Sebastian characterizes Olivia's mistake as natural since she was attracted to Cesario's masculine exterior.

Seeing a chance for his own happiness, the Duke shows interest in Cesario. Cesario accepts because she did, in fact, fall in love with him. The Duke wishes to see the Viola beneath the Cesario.

Olivia then requests to see Malvolio, at which point the Clown enters with his letter. Feste continues to ascribe madness to Malvolio. Irked by his unusual manner of reading the letter, Olivia asks Fabian to read it. The letter blames Olivia for the cruel joke that's been played on him. Though her love letter led him astray, he still kept his wits about him. He intends to broadcast the wrong she's done him. Olivia requests to see him.

The Duke proposes to Viola.

Malvolio enters chastising Olivia. She need only read her letter for the proof. Malvolio asked what possessed her to stoop to such a wicked scheme. Olivia recognizes the handwriting as Maria's and assures Malvolio that he will get justice. Fabian confesses his and the others' wrongdoing. He attributes their actions to "some stubborn and uncourteous parts," character flaws in them. Now that the trick has been exposed, Malvolio vows revenge on all those involved. Olivia acknowledges the abuse he's suffered at her servants' hands.

The Duke desires that a solemn combination be made of their hearts at a propitious hour. The third couple to join the other two is Maria and Sir Toby. Sir Toby proposed to Maria as a reward for her cleverness.

Analysis

This is the last scene of the play, so Shakespeare must provide a sense of closure. The way the action wraps up determines the overall meaning of the play. The genre of comedy has already provided us with some sense of the play's message. The dizzying sequence of interludes mirrors the festive form of the previous acts and gives the impression of a large holiday gathering. This scene is a fitting conglomeration of the play's elements—all the more satisfying because it resolves previous misunderstandings and complications. It ends in a happy "combination" of three couples. Even Malvolio is presented with some consolation from Olivia.

The Clown's irreverence toward the Duke is entirely in character. He is a wit to the very end. The Duke, pleased with his foolery, tips him twice before he goes off to get Olivia.

Antonio is necessary as a catalyst to the recognition scene. Having already raised hope of Sebastian's existence for Cesario, in this scene, Antonio dramatizes the duality of character. He speaks to Cesario as though he were Sebastian, which astonishes Cesario. The twins look alike, but they are not the same person. Antonio's previous dealings have been with Sebastian.

When Olivia enters, the Duke speaks the last words of love to her that he will ever speak. She has remained steadfast in her rejection. He acknowledges how futile his passion has been.

The confusion over mistaken identities continues a bit longer as Cesario prepares to leave with Orsino. Olivia speaks to Cesario as though he were her husband. This causes more astonishment for the Duke and Cesario—clarification has not yet come. The priest adds to the confusion by confirming the marriage ceremony between Sebastian and Olivia.

Happily the moment of recognition and resolution comes when Sebastian himself enters hard on the heels of Sir Andrew and Sir Toby. The twins, now together for the first time in the play, face each other and make their relationship clear. They are brother and sister. This clarification paves the way for the pairing of Viola and the Duke: "You shall from this time be/Your master's mistress." Critics offer numerous opinions on this ending. Alexander Leggat affirms that the play embodies the theme of love: "The ending takes little account of the reasons for particular attachments; it is, on the contrary, a generalized image of love." The pairings make up a formal design, which, in turn, illustrates the theme.

The cruel scheme against Malvolio is also laid bare in this scene. Fabian reads Malvolio's letter in which he accuses Olivia of abuse. Knowing herself innocent, Olivia requests to see Malvolio. When Malvolio comes, Olivia has a chance to vindicate herself and assign the blame to Maria where it belongs, for she composed the letter. Once again, this resolution, which may perhaps be cathartic for Malvolio, becomes a perverse reflection of the resolution of the love plot. Olivia tries to console him with the prospect of justice being served, while Malvolio, more harshly, thirsts for revenge.

Feste ends the play with a song, which unlike previous examples, has a looser connection to the action. The fact that the rain comes down every day has a bearing on their lives and activities. By referring to life's stages and natural imagery, he places the action in a larger, more ambiguous context. The song tells us how we are to take all the confusion and how we are to react to it. We shouldn't take troubles too seriously; life works itself out. The song is nonetheless open to interpretation. One critic has said of it that it is just "whistling in the dark."

Study Questions

1. Whose letter does Feste refuse to show Fabian?
2. With what disparaging term does the Clown refer to himself and Fabian?
3. Whom does Antonio think Cesario is?
4. Why does Olivia call in the priest?
5. What has happened to Sir Andrew?
6. What does Sebastian's presence signal?
7. Whom does Malvolio cast blame on in his letter?
8. With Olivia and Sebastian being the first couple, who make up the second couple?
9. Who make up the third pairing?
10. What satisfaction does Malvolio want for the trick?

Answers

1. Feste refuses to show Malvolio's letter.
2. The Clown refers to Fabian and himself as Olivia's "trappings."
3. Antonio thinks Cesario is Sebastian.
4. Olivia calls in the priest to verify her marriage to Sebastian.
5. Sir Andrew has been injured by Sebastian.
6. Sebastian's presence signals the resolution of the mistaken identity plot.
7. Malvolio casts blame on Olivia.
8. The second couple consists of the Duke and Viola.

9. Sir Toby and Maria make up the third couple.

10. Malvolio desires revenge on all his malefactors.

Suggested Essay Topics

1. Explain Antonio's function in the play. Is he a minor or major character? Does he clarify or interpret what is going on with the twins? Does he oppose or support the twins?

2. Isolate the methods that Shakespeare uses to establish and reveal character. It would probably be best to do a character study of one particular character. Are the actions of the characters properly motivated and consistent?

SECTION SEVEN

Bibliography

Abrams, M.H. *A Glossary of Literary Terms*. New York: Holt, Rinehart and Winston, 1981.

Barber, C.L. *Shakespeare's Festive Comedy*. Princeton: Princeton University Press, 1959.

Berry, Ralph. *Shakespeare's Comedies*. Princeton: Princeton University Press, 1972.

Brown, John. R. *Shakespeare and His Comedies*. London: Methuen & Co., Ltd., 1957.

Charney, Maurice. *All of Shakespeare*. New York: Columbia University Press, 1993.

Frye, Northrop. *Anatomy of Criticism*. Princeton: Princeton University Press, 1957.

Gaylin, Willard. *Rediscovering Love*. New York: Viking Penguin, Inc., 1986.

Leggatt, Alexander. *Shakespeare's Comedy of Love*. London: Methuen & Co., Ltd., 1974.

Levin, Richard. *Love and Society in Shakespearean Comedy*. Newark: University of Delaware Press, 1985.

Randle, John. *Understanding Britain*. Oxford: Basil Blackwell Publisher, 1981.

Schultz, Harold J. *History of England*. New York: Harper & Row, 1980.

Swinden, Patrick. *An Introduction to Shakespeare's Comedies*. London: The Macmillan Press, Ltd., 1973.

Encyclopedias

Britannica. Volume 27. Chicago: Encyclopedia Britannica, 1993, pp. 253–262.

Parrot, Thomas Marc. "William Shakespeare." *Collier's Encyclopedia*. New York: P.F. Collier, 1992, pp. 631–636.

Smith, Hallet. "William Shakespeare." *Encyclopedia Americana*. Danbury: Grolier Incorporated, 1994, pp. 652–659.

DOVER·THRIFT·EDITIONS

PLAYS

ANTIGONE, Sophocles. (0-486-27804-2)

AS YOU LIKE IT, William Shakespeare. (0-486-40432-3)

CYRANO DE BERGERAC, Edmond Rostand. (0-486-41119-2)

A DOLL'S HOUSE, Henrik Ibsen. (0-486-27062-9)

DR. FAUSTUS, Christopher Marlowe. (0-486-28208-2)

FIVE COMIC ONE-ACT PLAYS, Anton Chekhov. (0-486-40887-6)

FIVE GREAT COMEDIES, William Shakespeare. (0-486-44086-9)

FIVE GREAT GREEK TRAGEDIES, Sophocles, Euripides and Aeschylus. (0-486-43620-9)

FOUR GREAT HISTORIES, William Shakespeare. (0-486-44629-8)

FOUR GREAT RUSSIAN PLAYS, Anton Chekhov, Nikolai Gogol, Maxim Gorky, and Ivan Turgenev. (0-486-43472-9)

FOUR GREAT TRAGEDIES, William Shakespeare. (0-486-44083-4)

GHOSTS, Henrik Ibsen. (0-486-29852-3)

HAMLET, William Shakespeare. (0-486-27278-8)

HENRY V, William Shakespeare. (0-486-42887-7)

AN IDEAL HUSBAND, Oscar Wilde. (0-486-41423-X)

THE IMPORTANCE OF BEING EARNEST, Oscar Wilde. (0-486-26478-5)

JULIUS CAESAR, William Shakespeare. (0-486-26876-4)

KING LEAR, William Shakespeare. (0-486-28058-6)

LOVE'S LABOUR'S LOST, William Shakespeare. (0-486-41929-0)

LYSISTRATA, Aristophanes. (0-486-28225-2)

MACBETH, William Shakespeare. (0-486-27802-6)

MAJOR BARBARA, George Bernard Shaw. (0-486-42126-0)

MEDEA, Euripides. (0-486-27548-5)

THE MERCHANT OF VENICE, William Shakespeare. (0-486-28492-1)

A MIDSUMMER NIGHT'S DREAM, William Shakespeare. (0-486-27067-X)

MUCH ADO ABOUT NOTHING, William Shakespeare. (0-486-28272-4)

OEDIPUS REX, Sophocles. (0-486-26877-2)

THE ORESTEIA TRILOGY, Aeschylus. (0-486-29242-8)

OTHELLO, William Shakespeare. (0-486-29097-2)

THE PLAYBOY OF THE WESTERN WORLD AND RIDERS TO THE SEA, J. M. Synge. (0-486-27562-0)

DOVER · THRIFT · EDITIONS

PLAYS

PYGMALION, George Bernard Shaw. (0-486-28222-8)

ROMEO AND JULIET, William Shakespeare. (0-486-27557-4)

THE TAMING OF THE SHREW, William Shakespeare. (0-486-29765-9)

TARTUFFE, Molière. (0-486-41117-6)

THE TEMPEST, William Shakespeare. (0-486-40658-X)

TWELFTH NIGHT; OR, WHAT YOU WILL, William Shakespeare. (0-486-29290-8)

RICHARD III, William Shakespeare. (0-486-28747-5)

HEDDA GABLER, Henrik Ibsen. (0-486-26469-6)

THE COMEDY OF ERRORS, William Shakespeare. (0-486-42461-8)

THE CHERRY ORCHARD, Anton Chekhov. (0-486-26682-6)

SHE STOOPS TO CONQUER, Oliver Goldsmith. (0-486-26867-5)

THE WILD DUCK, Henrik Ibsen. (0-486-41116-8)

THE WINTER'S TALE, William Shakespeare. (0-486-41118-4)

ARMS AND THE MAN, George Bernard Shaw. (0-486-26476-9)

EVERYMAN, Anonymous. (0-486-28726-2)

THE FATHER, August Strindberg. (0-486-43217-3)

R.U.R., Karel Capek. (0-486-41926-6)

THE BEGGAR'S OPERA, John Gay. (0-486-40888-4)

3 BY SHAKESPEARE, William Shakespeare. (0-486-44721-9)

PROMETHEUS BOUND, Aeschylus. (0-486-28762-9)

REA's Study Guides

Review Books, Refreshers, and Comprehensive References

Problem Solvers®

Presenting an answer to the pressing need for easy-to-understand and up-to-date study guides detailing the wide world of mathematics and science.

High School Tutors®

In-depth guides that cover the length and breadth of the science and math subjects taught in high schools nationwide.

Essentials®

An insightful series of more useful, more practical, and more informative references comprehensively covering more than 150 subjects.

Super Reviews®

Don't miss a thing! Review it all thoroughly with this series of complete subject references at an affordable price.

Interactive Flashcard Books®

Flip through these essential, interactive study aids that go far beyond ordinary flashcards.

Reference

Explore dozens of clearly written, practical guides covering a wide scope of subjects from business to engineering to languages and many more.